AF256830

Me and My Hittas 5

A Novel by

Tranay Adams

Me And My Hittas 5

ISBN: 978-1-7377789-9-8

Email: dopereadzpresents@gmail.com

Facebook: Tranay Adams

Instagram: Tranay Adams

Cover Artist: Divine

PROLOGUE

"Damn, this shit here off the hook." Chingo blinked his glassy eyes and thumbed his nose. He was sitting at a table hunched over a half done line of heroin. His plug, Sazoo, stood beside him gripping the back of his chair.

"You like dat, huh?" A smile stretched across Sazoo's face. "Dis dat new sheet I'm fucking weet; fresh off dee wahta. Dis muddafucka pure as virgin pussy," He said in a thick African accent, jabbing the punctured packaged of heroin that lie on the table. He was a tall ass nigga, with jet black skin. Nigga damn near looked purple. His facial features were high cheek bones, a wide flat nose and big lips. At the moment he was wearing a Dashiki and sandals. Both of his pinky nails were long; he used either of them to snort his drug of choice.

"So what's cracking, cuz, you getting outta the coke game or what?" he laid back in the chair, getting all relaxed and shit.

"Noooooo," Sazoo shut his eyes and shook his head. "I could neva turn my back on her. She's been too good to me. I'm just curious to find out wut wealth dis stuff will bring me, ya undastand?"

Chingo nodded, wiping his dripping nose with a napkin.

"I can't front. That's some A1 shit chu got there, my nigga." Chingo pointed to the punctured package of heroin.

"Yeah," Sazoo swirled the dark liquor around in his glass, holding it near his lips. "I just gotta find me someone dat can move it. Big Brudda, if you know anyone dat might be interested in copping some of dee finest dope money can buy, you be sure to send 'em my way, eh?"

Sazoo patted him on the back.

"Shit, I'm interested," Chingo admitted.

At that moment, Sazoo was taking a sip from the glass and his brows rose. He brought the glass down from his mouth and licked his lips.

"What chu know 'bout heroin, Neega?"

Chingo held his hands out before his eyes, looking between them both.

These hands have moved coke, dope, weed, hash, X and so more shit." Chingo relayed. He had his hands out before him like they possessed some kind of myskital powers of some shit."I'ma hustla, my nigga; I could sell a big screen TV to a blind man."

Chingo took a sip from his glass of Hennessy.

"Confidence, I like dat." He nodded, impressed with his attitude.

"On some real shit, Zoo, I can move this dope. The Bottoms are an open market for this shit right now."

"There's no H on your side of the fence?" his forehead wrinkled.

"Yeah, there's some H by my way. I mean, if you wanna call it that. These dudes done ran the fiends off with that garbage they're pushing. But with yo shit, I'm positive that I can get 'em back."

Sazoo massaged his chin as he thought on it, eyes staring out of their corners.

"Hmmmm, I tell ya wut, since you're so sure; I'm going to give you an ounce of it." Sazoo told him. "You see wut it does on your end. And if the chickens get ta clucking, I'll set chu out wit a sweet price per kilo, how 'bout dat?"

"How much are we talking?"

The African grabbed a napkin and scribbled down a couple of numbers. He then slid the napkin before Chingo. When Chingo saw the quote, his eyes bulged and he whistled.

He took a sip of his drink and said, "Oh, yeah, I can most definitely fuck with this. You gone let me get that ounce up out cha 'fore I leave?"

Sazoo nodded and went about the business of packaging up the heroin he was going to give to Chingo.

Later that night

Leroy was on his feet with his eyes closed and his hands in his pockets, leaning forward. Just when it looked like he was going to fall flat on his face his body would lean in another direction. He'd been at it for a time, leaning at different angles but never falling. You'd think he was a puppet being held by invisible strings if you didn't know any better. When Chingo sent a couple of his little homies into the streets to find a fiend to test his heroin out on, there weren't a shortage of volunteers. The dope heads had their hands raised high and were jumping up and down as if they were a couple of kids eager to be picked by their teacher. When the little homies decided on Leroy he danced around and shouted as if he had the winning numbers of a multimillion lottery ticket.

He felt like it was one of the luckiest days of his life being that he hadn't had a fix in a while and was starting to feel sick. Leroy had just stolen a cap gun from out of the local 99 cents store and spray painted it black. Later on that night he had planned on holding up a liquor store to support his habit, but now all of that had changed and he was on his way to getting a free shot. He had only hoped that the dope was as sweet as the young boys had said it was. Little did old Leroy know he was in for a treat; as soon as that needle pierced his vein and he pushed that poison into his bloodline he fell in love. The drug's potency hurtled him back into the 70s where it was a little easier to find superior dope. A movie played behind his eyelids and he saw himself as a kid again.

It was the summer of '74 and the temperature was a sweltering 97 degrees. All of the neighborhood kids were running back and forth in the streets, throwing water balloons and shooting water guns at one another. A smile stretched across Leroy's face as he thought about how good the water felt when it splashed against his scrawny body that day. He was just a little nigga then, a ten year old boy. That was many sunrises ago but you couldn't tell him that he wasn't living through that experience at this very moment.

"Man, look at this mothafucka." One of the little homies said amused, watching Leroy in his dope fiend lean.

"Cuz leaning like Michael Jackson in the Smooth Criminal music video." Another one of the little homies said.

Chingo was leaning against the doorway of the kitchen with his elbow resting in the palm of his hand while his other hand massaged his chin. His eyes were focused on Leroy and his reaction to the dope. He'd seen niggaz on dope lean before but none of them leaned quite like the old head did. The way Leroy was going at it, it reminded him of Neo in The Matrix when he was on that roof with Agent Smith and he was letting that hammer go on him. Neo had seen those bullets coming at him in slow motion and leaned all of the way back to avoid them. It was like he was doing the limbo under an invisible stick or shit. That's when a thought struck Chingo like a spear. Good dope needed a good name, an official name so its buyers could distinguish it from other products. A good name could snag a fiend's curiosity. A grin surfaced on the hustler's face. He stood up straight and snapped his fingers. Eureka.

"I got it, Cuz!" He announced to his little homies as he entered the living room where they were watching Leroy in his lean.

"What? Gonorrhea?" one of the little homies asked over his shoulder, causing everyone to bust up laughing. A couple of the other homies slapped hands with him, giving him props on the funny joke.

Chingo shot the youth a dangerous look and the living room suddenly got quiet and serious. Once he saw that the others knew that he wasn't in the mood to fuck around, he continued on with what he had to say.

"We're gone call this shit," he scribbled on one of the small envelopes with a black Sharpie marker and held it up. "The Matrix, 'cause it's gone have the heads leaning."

"Hell yeah!" said one of the homies.

"That's what's up!" said another.

"The Matrix!" someone else cosigned.

Seeing that his homies were feeling the name, Chingo nodded his head. He packaged two more of the small envelopes with the heroin and sealed them shut.

"Ay, one of y'all niggaz wake old head up." Chingo said, as he took a glass down from the cupboard and filled it with faucet water.

"Say, Cuz, wake yo ass up!" he heard one of the little homies holler at Leroy. The next thing he heard was...

Smack!

"Huh, what the fuck is going on?" Leroy rubbed his stinging cheek, looking around like he didn't know what the fuck hit him.

"Have a seat," Chingo pointed to the chair behind Leroy as he approached with a glass of water. Once he'd sat down he passed him the glass of water. He watched the old dope head drink half of it down before kneeling before him. He held the two small envelopes up so Leroy could see them, before he began.

"These two are for you, Old Head..." He told him. When Leroy went to pluck the envelopes from Chingo's fingers he snatched them back. "On one condition, I want chu to make the other heads out there well aware of the nigga that's holding this good dope. You spread the word, Cuz. You let 'em know that The Matrix is the product that they need to be fucking with. I got a pack for every head you bring back, you hear me?"

Leroy sat up, eyes bulging and licking his ashy, chapped lips. The mention of more of that sweet dope made him look alive.

"You got it, Chingo." Leroy eyed the envelopes hungrily. "I'ma have an army of dope fiends at this bitch. I hope you ready 'cause it's gone look like Night of the Living Dope Fiends out this mothafucka. Trust and believe that."

Chingo relinquished the two envelopes to Leroy and he hurriedly got to his feet. He gathered the utensils he used to shoot up with and stuffed them into a worn black leather bag. He slapped a trucker cap on his nappy head and limped to the door on his prosthetic leg.

"You just wait Chingo, you gone be one rich ass nigga when I'm through advertising out here," Leroy swore. "You just watch and see, youngster."

Chingo had a devilish smile etched on his face when he turned to his little homies, rubbing his hands together greedily.

"It's on now, my niggaz."

Boc! Boc! Boc! Poc! Poc! Boc!

Bop! Poc! Poc! Bop!

The windows imploded as bullets whizzed through them, raining shards everywhere. Chingo and the homies dove to the floor narrowly avoiding the bullets that were meant to take their lives. Once they heard the squealing of tires, they hurriedly hopped to their feet and retrieved their weapons. They were about to sprint out of the house when they noticed one of the homies sitting in the La-Z-Boy reclining chair. He looked like he was just fine until Chingo further examined him. His head was turned to the side. His eyes were rolled to their corners and his mouth was a gap. The front of his tank top was full of bleeding, gaping holes.

"Damn, Cuz," one of the little homies said, "They got Lil' Cartoon."

"Fuck man!" another one of the little homies chimed in, gripping the sides of his head.

The sound of a man groaning drew every ones attention outside. Chingo unlocked and unchained the door. He snatched the door open and was the first man out. He rushed over to Leroy who was stretched out on the lawn, lying flat on his back. A gaping hole was at the center of his chest and a mask of excruciation was painted on his face. Hearing someone approaching, Leroy's eyes peeled open and tears ran from the corners of them.

"Young blood, I'm finished, Man," Leroy told Chingo. "I can't feel shit from the neck down. I'll never walk again; I can't live like this, Bruh. Not like this." He trailed off whimpering and crying. Seeing the old head like this fucked with Chingo's mental. He hated to see a civilian suffering on the account of a beef that was his own.

"You gone be all right, G, we just gotta get chu to the 'spital." Chingo pulled out his cell phone. He was about to call 9-1-1 when Leroy stopped him.

"Nah, nah, nah, they take me to the hospital and I'ma go through detox." Leroy told him. "I'ma be cramping and throwing up like some sick fucking dog. I can't fade that. I'm telling you, Young blood, you gone have to finish me. I can't go on like this here. Please." The tears seemed to pour from the corners of his eyes. This predicament had reduced a grown man to sounding like a scared little girl.

"All right, G, if that's how you want it." Chingo told him. "Close your eyes. Now relax, breathe easy." He pressed his bangers into Leroy's left breast where his beating heart resided. He then took a deep breath and pulled the trigger. The sudden blast caused Leroy's body to jerk violently. Chingo stood to his feet and looked over his handiwork. Afterwards, he treaded past his homies and into the house.

Chingo realized that the only way he was going to get back into the hustle and bustle of things is when the war was over. Otherwise, he may as well pack up his operation and move it out of The Low Bottoms. He couldn't see himself getting a dollar somewhere else. He loved his soil too much. He didn't know how yet, but some way he was going to put an end to the killings. He had, too. He had family and friends counting on him.

ONE

Pavielle looked up into the sky as the doves were released at the cemetery for Gangsta's funeral. Everyone had come out to show the O.G shot-caller love. Homies in red garments were in clusters amongst the mourners. There were also some of them sprinkled throughout the crowd. Most of them wore R.I.P T-shirts with a young Gangsta on the front of them striking a gangster pose and throwing up the set. Others wore fresh ink on their forearms and chests; *T.I.P Big Gangsta* along with his birth and passing date was tattooed into their flesh. Some of the homies and homegirls cried while others wore hard-faces or adopted black shades to hide the heartache in their eyes. Throughout the funeral Pavielle heard a few of the homies whispering about how they were going to put in work and ride in honor of Gangsta. Pavielle hoped that they weren't just talking out of their asses, because as new leader of the set he was going to put in the order to have everyone murdered that held any affiliation with Paybacc.

As Pavielle watched Gangsta's blood red coffin be lowered into the ground, he knew that he would never be the same. When Gangsta had departed this world for the next he took a piece of Pavielle with him. Pavielle knew that it was a piece that he'd never get back until that one day came when they would be reunited. Once dirt had begun to be shoveled onto Gangsta's coffin, Pavielle slid on his black sunglasses and walked away, taking an army of red clad soldiers along with him.

"I won't this nigga's set hit every night, if niggaz tuck their tail and stay inside then we start hitting they ass in broad daylight. I don't give a fuck! Cock sucka stole my uncle from me; took the realest nigga to ever breathe air outta this world!

I don't have no sympathy for nobody! Five bodies," Pavielle held up both hand, his hateful eyes looking at the men surrounding him. "I want a minimum of five bodies a night. If I catch wind that one of the homies isn't putting in any work, then they're dead out here. They can't get money in The Bottoms no more, period. You gone have to pack up and get your hustle on over there on the Westside or some shit," Pavielle lay back in his chair and lit up a blunt. He took a pull and blew the smoke back out. He looked around at all of the faces that occupied the living room. "Fuck y'all niggaz waiting on? Get the fuck outta here and make them bitch ass niggaz feel it." With that said, everyone filed out of the room and out of the door.

Sitting at the rectangle shaped black wood table alone, Pavielle poured himself a glass of Cognac. He took another pull from his blunt and blew out smoke before taking a casual sip from the glass. Since Gangsta had been murdered he'd changed, and it hadn't gone un-noticed by his loved ones. He'd become angrier and more ruthless; a ruthlessness that up until now only Paybacc possessed. Not only had Pavielle's personality changed, but his outward appearance did as well. He rocked a 5 o'clock shadow and his new growth was pushing his fuzzy braids up from their roots. He had black bags under his eyes and he drunk hard liquor as if it was water. His normally slender body had become skinny and frail in appearance. He hardly ever ate. If he wasn't taking a bottle of something to the head then he was putting weed smoke into the air.

Gouch came out of the study and pulled out a chair beside Pavielle. Pavielle passed him the blunt and he took a couple of pulls. He blew the smoke out of the corner of his mouth and scratched his temple with his thumb.

"I just got off the jack with Jesus; he said he's sending some of his hardest hitters out here. He said he has an army of cut throat Mexicans that he's flying out that can help us put the smash down. He said they should be arriving here tomorrow night and that he'd give us a call once…"

"You call Jesus back and tell him I said thanks but no thanks. I don't need his help. I got this." Pavielle poured himself another glass of Cognac. "I'ma grown ass man, I don't need him playing my daddy. This is my problem and I'ma take care of it."

"Yo, Booby, man. Maybe you should consider the offer. I mean, a couple of mo' guns won't hurt. The more the merrier."

"I'm the head of this empire and this set." Pavielle began, picking up his glass. "When it's your time to wear this crown, then you run this kingdom how you see fit. Until that day comes, I'm rocking this bitch how I wanna, you Griff me?"

Gouch glared at Pavielle and balled his fists tight. He was so angry that the corner of his mouth twitched. He could feel the blood inside of him boiling. It took all he had to stop himself from beating the brakes off his baby brother. He'd let him slide because he knew that they both were dealing with the lost of Gangsta. He understood that Pavielle's behavior and slick mouth was his way of coping with the pain.

"Nigga, why are you still here?" Pavielle spat, arching his eyebrows.

Gouch brought his hand down his face and blew hard. He took another pull from the blunt before mashing it out into the ashtray. He rose to his feet and headed back into the study to call Black Jesus back. Pavielle stood erect and walked over to the window. He held back the curtain and peered outside. His eyes swept back and forth across the 20,000 acre estate that Gangsta had been left him in his will as he sipped on Cognac.

Feeling movement at his rear, Pavielle whipped around pulling his black .9mm. Vayda jumped back with her hand over her heart, startled by her fiance's sudden movement and the appearance of his gun. Seeing that it was just his wife to be, Pavielle tucked the black .9mm into his waistline and turned his attention back to the window. Vayda sauntered across the hardwood floor, her mint green Victoria Secret gown drifting along the way. She wrapped her arms around Pavielle's waist and laid her head against his back. For a time she listened to his heart beat and the sound of his breathing.

"When are you coming to bed?" Vayda asked.

"I'm not sleepy," Pavielle answered, never taking his eyes from the window.

"Who said anything about sleeping?" she grinned and grabbed the bulge in his jeans; the kyoung kingpin didn't even flinch.

"I'm not in the mood." He replied roughly, grabbing Vayda by the wrist and pulling her hand away from his crotch.

"Well, you can just come up stairs and we can just talk. I know you probably have a lot on your mind that you wanna…"

"Get off my back," Pavielle said to her, before taking a sip from his glass of Cognac.

"What?" she frowned.

Pavielle whipped around to Vayda. "I said get off my back! I just came outta coma from being shot! I lost my uncle! Countless homies, and on top of that I gotta watch my back and make sure this psycho doesn't whack what lil' family I do have left! So, no! I don't wanna talk! I don't wanna be sucked and I sure as hell don't wanna be fucked! All I want to be is left alone, Jesus-H-fucking Christ!" He threw the glass of Cognac at Vayda's head and she ducked. The glass exploded when it struck the wall and its contents soaked into the carpet. The noise awoke the baby and he cried aloud. Vayda stood there staring at Pavielle for a while before storming off up the stairs to the baby's bedroom.

Gouch stepped back into the dining room. He looked from the broken glass on the carpet to Pavielle, then up the stairs where he saw Vayda disappear through the doorway of the baby's bedroom. It wasn't hard for him to come to a conclusion of what had just occurred.

"I put the call through to Black Jesus and he didn't seem too happy about it. He made me promise to have you have a sit-down with him." He poured up another glass of alcohol.

"He wants a sit-down? Fine; let him come to me. I'm not making the trip; he's not the only boss in Cali." Pavielle swirled the dark liquor around in his glass.

"I'm outta here, Man." Gouch told Pavielle before heading for the front door.

"Where you going? Get over here." Pavielle sat his glass down and opened his arms for an embrace. Gouch embraced his baby brother not really wanting to since he was still pissed off at him. "I love you." He kissed Gouch on the cheek.

"I know," Gouch responded dryly and left the mansion.

5

TWO

Voodoo pushed an old Volvo station wagon through the streets blasting 50 cent's Heat. She and Dip passed a bottle of Gin and orange juice between themselves. They were high and liquored up, like they always were when they were on a mission to do the Devil's work. Through glassy, red eyes Dip kept a look out for any police cars that may be out on patrol. They were in a G-ride (a stolen car) and weren't trying to get knocked by The Rollers before they carried out their assignment.

Keep thinking I'm candy 'til your fucking skull get popped/ and your brain jump out the top like Jack in the Box/ In the hood summer time it's killing season/ It's hot out this bitch that's a good enough reason...

Voodoo sang along with 50 cent as he spat over the Dr. Dre produced track. She was a caramel skinned chick born in Trinidad and raised in The Low Bottoms. She rocked her dark brown hair in short dreadlocks and boasted a tattoo in Old English letters across her forehead: Outlaws. Two red tear drops were inked at the corner of her right-eye. Though a female, Voodoo, went just as hard as any of the men from the set, which is why she had their respect.

"Voodoo, you mind turning that shit down? Damn, you're gonna get us knocked before we get to the mothafucka." G-thang said, with a hard-face from the backseat. He had loaded a banana clip into his AK-47. He was a tall, thin cat who sported his hair like O-Dog in Menace II Society. He had dark, blotched skin and nappy facial hair. He was 28 years old, but his face was the mask of a man twice that age. His dark eyes told a story that belonged behind the cover of a Sapphire novel.

Voodoo turned the stereo down and looked at G-thang through the rearview mirror. "You say something, Blood?" she asked, not hearing him over the loud music.

"Turn that shit down!" G-thang barked. "Matter of fact, turn that bullshit off." Voodoo sucked her teeth and turned the stereo all the way up. She saw G-thang saying something through the rearview mirror but she couldn't hear him because the music was too loud. From his glassy eyes and the spittle flying from his lips, she could tell that he was pissed but she didn't give a fuck. Gangsters did what they wanted and busters did what they could. G-thang leaned up front, ejected the CD, and threw it out of the window.

"What the fuck is your problem?" Voodoo spat at G-thang.

"You think this shit is a game, Blood? We're about to commit murder; a gang of'em. We riding with some thangs that could get the both of y'all 10 years flat, and me life being that I'ma convicted felon. I'm not tryna get pulled over by Binem with these tools on me. I'm telling you now; I'm not going back to the joint. I'll bang it out with them boys before the state sees me."

"Whatever, nigga," Voodoo turned up the 5th of Seagram's Gin, her throat moving up and down her neck as she guzzled it. She wiped her mouth and passed the bottle off to Dip.

"Whatever my ass, I'm not about to get cased up on the account of you."

"Y'all bitches chill, fam, ain't nobody gone get knocked." Dip swore, holding the bottle near his lips. "We gone roll over into these niggaz hood and drop the lot of'em.

It's as simple as that. Buck these ho ass niggaz down then take it back to the set." He finally took a swig from the Seagram bottle. He then passed it over his shoulder to G-thang, who took it to the head. At 22 years old Dip was the youngest of the threesome. He had a talent for doing dirt and a hunger for hood stardom. It was that appetite for destruction that catapulted him to G status. "Yo, Voodoo, kill dem lights. This is it right here." Dip pointed to the windshield at a brown and tan Spanish stucco house.

Voodoo stopped the car in the middle of the street and executed its headlights, letting its engine idle. G-thang and Dip zipped their LRG hoodies up to their heads. Their domes were completely covered but their eyes were visible through the eye slots in them. The twosome cocked the hammers on their assault rifles and stepped out into the night. Instantly, their noses were assaulted by the strong scent of marijuana. They could hear the loud music coming from the backyard of the brown and tan house as a party was going on. They tucked their weapons to their persons, hunched over and moved towards the brick fence of the house. G-thang headed into the alley and snuck a peek through the backyard gate of the house. Homies and homegirls of the Eastside Crip card were drinking, smoking and dancing. Everyone seemed to be having a good old time; oblivious to the chaos that was about to be unleashed upon them.

G-thang poked his head out of the alley looking for Dip. He spotted the youngster rolling a trashcan over to the fence of the house. Once he climbed on top of it and hunched down, he gave G-thang a nod. G-thang held up three fingers signaling for them to start the shooting at the count of three. Once his last finger dropped, he swung into the alley with his AK pointed into the backyard. Dip stood erect on the trashcan. Together they pulled the triggers of their weapons, causing fire to spit from them. The twosome cut loose and watched the expressions of shock and pain registered on their targets faces. Some ran, some tried to take cover, some even tried to return fire, but eventually they all fell victim to the assault rifles bullets. G-thang and Dip released the triggers of their weapons and the barrels of them smoked like a burnt turkey. They took the time to admire their handiwork as they removed the empty banana clips from their weapons and injected new ones. There was a collage of dead bodies strewn on the ground; some of them over lapping one another. The bullet riddled forms were covered in holes and crimson stains. Now that the noise of men and women having a good time was gone, all that could be heard was 2pac's Gangsta Party blaring from the speakers.

Dip looked to the DJ and he was slumped behind the turntable with a row of bleeding black holes across his chest. Dip aimed his AK at the turntable and shot it up along with the speakers, disabling the music. Out the corner of his eye he saw a flicker of movement. He turned around and saw a poor soul squirming underneath a pile of bodies with his hand outstretched.

"Come on, Blood! Let's go!" G-thang hollered to Dip.

"Hold on, nigga!" Dip shouted back before jumping down into the mess of corpses. He moved through the maze of bodies until he reached the squirming individual. He moved the dead persons from off of him and found a man gasping for air. For a moment Dip stared at him, then he raised his AK and blasted apart his skull and face. The man went limp and his hand dropped.

"What the fuck are y'all niggaz doing, Blood?!" Voodoo yelled out.

"Nigga, come the fuck on!" she heard G-thang yell.

Hearing a plastic cup fall to his right, Dip swung around squeezing the trigger of his AK. Sparks and metal flew from the iron door and a little girl was cut down in the doorway of the back porch. She collapsed where she stood; her small frame littered with holes and her Sponge Bob pajamas a bloody mess. Dip's heart dropped and a look of surprise masked his face. He stood over the little girl as she gasped for breath, clinging for dear life. Her tiny hand reached out for Dip's hand wanting his help. Dip's eyes welled up with tears and they spilled down his cheeks. He went to reach for the little girl's hand. He'd almost grasped it when it suddenly fell to her side. The little girl stared wide eyed at nothing. She was looking off to the side when she gave her last breath. Her Teddy Bear, which was lying beside her, had been ruined by holes and its cotton stuffing had absorbed some of her blood.

Dip closed his eyes and shook his head; sadden by the horrible act that he'd just committed. He sniffled and wiped his tearing eyes with his gloved hand. He was so zoned out by the tragedy that he didn't even hear the police car sirens that were quickly approaching. In fact, he'd forgotten that he was standing in the middle of a massacre with dead bodies strewn all around. A strong hand pulled on his hoodie and snapped him back to reality. He swung around with his AK ready to let something fly, but when he saw that it was G-thang he lowered his weapon.

"Let's go, Blood!" G-thang spat. He whipped around to the gate and blasted away the chain that held it closed. He pulled it open and they spilled out into the alley and into the stolen Volvo. The Volvo raced down the alley kicking up dust and leaving papers floating in the air.

"Dip, what the fuck were you doing back there?" G-thang asked angrily.

"That's what the fuck I wanna know." Vayda said, commanding the whip. She was pissed off too; they couldn't have gotten knocked back there.

"I killed a lil' girl, I shot her up." Dip said, with glassy eyes.

G-thang and Voodoo exchanged glances. G-thang shook his head and brought a gloved hand down his face, hating to hear that a little girl had been murdered. "Shit!" he bellowed, pounding the dashboard in anger. Before he could vent any further red and blue lights flashed at the back of them, accompanied by a blaring siren. That eerie noise caused every ones stomachs to twists into knots.

"Shit! It's Binem!" Dip stole a glance out the back window. "Fuck are we gone do?"

"I ain't going to jail, Blood, I already done told y'all." G-thang exchanged knowing glances with everyone, getting a clear understanding about what was about to go down. After their respective nods were given, they all took a hold of their individual weapons. G-thang and Dip let down their windows just as Voodoo banked a right out of the alley. "Voodoo, when you reach the stop-sign slam on the brakes; me and Dip gone give these bitch-boys havoc."

"I got chu." Voodoo replied, a scowl fixed on her face. Reaching the stop-sign, she slammed on the brakes, causing the police car to slam into the back of them. Quickly, G-thang and Dip emerged out of their windows and pointed their AKs at the police car's windshield, spraying it up. The cops inside the police car shook like they were having a seizure as bullets burst through the windshield and chewed up their forms. Their blood splattered the inside of the cracked windshield and they killed over. G-thang and Dip ducked back into the Volvo and

Voodoo sped off. They bent the corner at the end of the block and a hubcap dislodged from the Volvo's back tire, rolling out into the street. A police car got behind them and G-thang and Dip came back out of the Volvo, banging holes through the hood and windshield of the police car. The police car lost control and crashed into a parked van.

Boof!

"Oh, fuck!" Voodoo cursed after going over a spike strip and hearing the tires blow out. She lost control of the vehicle and it slammed into a light-post, wrapping around it.

Voodoo peeled her forehead up from the steering-wheel, spilling blood. She glanced at the rearview mirror and blood was running down her face from a gash in her forehead. Seeing police cars racing towards them up ahead, she quickly shook G-thang and Dip from their daze. As soon as everyone hopped out of the car, the police cars skidded to a halt before them. The police were hopping out of their cars with their guns drawn, but the threesome releasing the fury of their AKs upon them made them take cover.

"Y'all cover me!" G-thang yelled to Voodoo and Dip. Voodoo and Dip ejected the empty banana clips from their AKs and injected full ones. While they held G-thang down, he whipped his AK around to the Volvo's gas-tank and pulled its trigger. The Volvo exploded in a roar of fire and black smoke, scattering wreckage everywhere. The diversion was just what the trio needed to make their escape.

THREE

Pavielle sat behind his green marble top desk in his executive chair. He slowly sipped Cognac as he stared at the 60 inch LED flat-screen. His dark, baggy eyes stared observantly at the scene playing out before him. His pet python slowly moved around in its aquarium creeping towards a white mouse that was desperately trying to escape the confines of its glass prison. The mouse must have felt its end hastily approaching, because its heart was beating so fast that it looked as if it were about to erupt out of its chest. Giving up on finding salvation, the mouse backed its self into the corner. Its beady red eyes stared at the python as it neared. You could practically smell the fear coming off of the rodent. Pavielle watched attentively as the python suddenly stopped, slithering its tongue. It just sat there for a moment, as if it were waiting for the mouse to make its move. Then suddenly, the python shot forward, clamping its powerful jaws around the mouse and wrapping its self around its body. The python squeezed with all of its might, oozing the life from the furry creature's form.

Pavielle held up his glass and said, "R.I.P Stewart Little. Sorry, Dawg. That's just how it is. Life's a bitch and then you die." He crossed his heart in the name of the Lord with one hand and used the other to take a sip of Cognac. He sat his glass down and watched as the python expanded its jaws in preparation to devour the mouse.

"Mr. Hood, Gouch and Killa Dre are here to see you." A voice came over the intercom.

Pavielle held down the button to the intercom and spoke, "Let'em in."

Pavielle casually took sips of Cognac as he watched the python swallow the mouse whole. Gouch entered the study with Killa Dre on his heels. Gouch sat on the edge of Pavielle's desk and Killa walked over to the aquarium. He kneeled down at eye level with the aquarium, looking from it to the tripod that held the video-camera that had been filming the entire ordeal. Killa Dre rose to his feet, walked over to the chair before Pavielle's desk and sat down.

"So, Mr. Gouch, what is it that I can do for you?" Pavielle asked.

"Nigga, you didn't see the news?" Gouch inquired. "G-thang, Dip,and Voodoo wet up some party the Eastside Crips threw and soaked up a couple of cops; shits on every news channel. I can't believe you haven't seen it." He picked up the remote control from off the desk and turned on the flat-screen, flipping through the channels until he found the news broadcast that he'd just told Pavielle about.

Police are calling this gruesome scene a massacre. A total of twenty-two people have been killed; seven men, nine women and a seven year old little girl. All shot down by AK-47 assault rifles. Authorities believe that the shooting was retaliation for the recent murders of Blood gang members, namely Charles 'Gangsta' Vines. The two gangs; the Eastside Crips and the Outlaws Rolling 20s Bloods are two rival gangs that have been a part of the ongoing color war since the late 60s, early 70s

Pavielle, Gouch and Killa Dre listened as the reporter went on to tell about the high speed chase that took place when the police tried to apprehend G-thang, Dip and Voodoo. They found out that G-thang and Dip had killed three police officers and had injured four others. Many of whom would have to have their limbs amputated due to them being mutilated beyond repair by assault rifle bullets. Once the report was over Gouch turned the TV down and turned to Pavielle.

"Damn, man," Gouch shook his head. "They winded up clipping that lil girl."

Pavielle shrugged and said, "People die every day, Gucci. She was a casualty of war." He took a sip of Cognac. Hearing Pavielle speak of a child being murdered so nonchalantly caused Gouch and Killa Dre to frown and exchange glances. Gouch looked at his baby brother like he was the Tin-Man from the Wizard of Oz. He didn't have a heart. Gouch was sure that there was an ice berg where his heart used to be.

"Fuck you looking at?" Pavielle asked Gouch, who shook his head, "Have you heard from G-thang and them?" he asked.

"Nah, I've been trying to reach them, but they're not picking up their phones." He informed him.

"Good, hopefully they got rid of them. Fucking cell phones are traps; Binem can use the GPS system in them to track niggaz down." Pavielle let him know.

"What's that light blinking for?" Killa Dre with a finger pointed at a red flashing bulb at the corner of the study. Pavielle looked to where Killa Dre was pointing then rose to his feet. He downed the last of the Cognac and sat the glass back down on the green marble top. He motioned for Gouch and Killa Dre to follow him as he headed out of the study. Pavielle pressed a code into a digital key-pad placed at the side of the basement door. There was a *Beep* and *Open* flashed on the screen of the digital key-pad. Pavielle held down the mechanism of the door handle and let himself inside of the basement. He made his way down the steps with Gouch and Killa Dre on his heels. On the way down the staircase they could hear a telephone ringing. The ringing stopped for a moment, and then it started back up again.

The mansion that Pavielle and his family now inhabited was purchased by Gangsta. He'd gotten an untraceable and completely private landline installed down in the basement. He'd used the line to discuss business that would surely have gotten him indicted or picked up on conspiracy charges. Gangsta left the house, amongst other assets, to Pavielle and Gouch in his will before he'd passed away. Gangsta had spoken of the telephone line on several occasions to Pavielle so he knew all about it and the purpose that it served.

After flipping on the light switch, Pavielle walked over to the telephone and picked up the receiver. He placed it to his ear and said, "Hello?" he wore a solemn face as he listened to what he was being told. "Yeah, the shit is all over the news; made every channel. Y'all got they hood live as a mothafucka. Listen, G, where are y'all at now? Alright, get a pen and write down this address." Pavielle gave G-thang an address. "That's a lil' spot I got out in Ladera Heights. Y'all find y'all way out there. Look under the Welcome Mat and you'll find the key there. Y'all sit tight until I figure out y'all next move. Yeah, most definitely, y'all are gonna have to leave the country. But don't trip, Duse Owe, I'ma set y'all up real nice and make sure y'all are straight. Peace." Pavielle hung up the phone and turned around to Gouch and Killa Dre.

"What's up with the homies?" Gouch inquired, folding his arms across his chest.

"They're holed up in Voodoo's girl's basement right now. I told them to get out to Ladera Heights to that house upon the hill I copped last summer for G-momma that she refused to live in. It's nice and quiet out there. They should be able to lay low for a minute until I figure out exactly what I plan to do with them."

"Man, they're some Hot Boys right about now." Killa Dre exclaimed, shaking his head shamefully. "Twenty-five bodies and three of 'em are Binem? Their faces are gonna be plastered on every news paper and channel in the next couple of days. The Ones are gonna have a nationwide manhunt for 'em. The homies are gonna have to get outta dodge, Blood, real soon. Before shit is sewn up so tight that they won't be able to leave the state."

"Killa is right, Bro. They're gonna have to leave soon if they expect to have a chance of making it outta the country. 'Cause God forbid if they were caught. They'd be looking at the death penalty or maybe something even worse if the cops decided to seek revenge, you Griff me?" Gouch said. Pavielle conceded.

"Call our guy, see if he can rustle up a few passports, I.Ds, and social security cards for 'em. They're gonna need new identities and plenty of paper; you can't go on the run without either one."

Gouch didn't waste any time whipping out his cell phone and punching in the number to the fellow that could help them with their crisis.

$$$

G-thang hung up the telephone and turned around to Voodoo and Dip. Voodoo was sitting on the La-Z-Boy taking swigs from a bottle of Remy Martin and Vida was sitting on her lap. Dip was sitting on a chair in the corner of the basement trying to suck the life out of a blunt, smoke wafting around him. It was his fourth one in the past hour and he didn't show any signs of slowing down. His eyes were red and lazy and he was more relaxed having ventured off on the herbal retreat. The effect of the Kush was very much needed after he'd bloodied his hands committing the despicable act. He had stolen a child's life and he was confident that in the next life he'd be bathed in the flaming waters of hell.

"What did he say for us to do, G?" Voodoo asked.

"He wants us to get out to Ladera Heights." G-thang answered. "Says he has a spot out there, he wants us to lay low for a while until he's able to get us outta the country." He took a pull from his cigarette and blew out a cloud of smoke. "If we're gonna be moving about on the streets I think we need to change our appearances."

"What do you suggest?" Voodoo asked, gripping Vida's thigh.

"I'ma cut my hair and shave my face clean." G-thang told them. "Dip, you shave yours bald. Voodoo, dye yours and have baby girl put 'em in cornrows or something. You're gonna have to put some makeup on to cover up those tattoos."

"Alright," Voodoo nodded her head and took a swig from the Remy bottle.

"Dip?" G-thang looked to his little homie. He was staring off into space in deep thought. "Yoooo!" He snapped his fingers and finally stole Dip's attention. The youth raised his eyebrows like 'What's up?' "Did you hear me?"

Dip nodded. "Yeah, I heard you; shave my head bald."

G-thang stepped to Dip and gripped his shoulder, staring him in his eyes. "Lil' Bruh, you gotta let that shit go or it's going to eat chu alive. Ain't nothing you can do about that. It happened and there is no changing it. You made a mistake; shit happens. In this thing of ours there are casualties of war, just like any other war, Homie. You wanna grieve? Alright cool, but do it once we're settled down outta the country, OK?" Dip nodded. "Alright, come on so I can shave that dome of yours." He ruffled Dip's head. The youth rose to his feet and he threw his arm over his shoulders. G-thang looked to Vida. "Yo, Vida, you got some clippers up stairs?"

"Uh huh," Vida said, in between kissing Voodoo, "Under the bathroom sink."

"Alright, G' looking," G-thang led Dip up the stairs.

FOUR

Nino pushed the tan Dodge Intrepid while his man Bebop rode shotgun. Both men were draped in all black, keeping an eye out for enemies deserving of the slugs loaded in the magazines of their Uzis.

"This block is like a mothafucking ghost town," Bebop said to no one in particular, "Where in the fuck are these clowns?"

"Ducking and hiding, Blood, they know them riders are out." Nino spoke.

"Well, they need to come out, you heard what the big homie said, 'he wants ten bodies a night', and I'm tryna meet my quota, feel me?"

Nino nodded his head.

"Who dat up there?" Bebop asked, staring through the windshield at a couple of neighborhood kids on a bicycle. One was peddling while the other was riding the handlebars. They couldn't have been any older than thirteen and fourteen years old. They didn't have on a blue garment between the two of them, so there was no way of telling if they were in the life. Unfortunately for them, the hood they were parlaying in just so happened to belong to Nino and Bebop's enemies.

"Just some lil' niggaz, man, they probably don't even bang." Nino waved the youngsters off. "I'ma roll up on 'em and see what's up, though."

"Nah, fuck all of that," Bebop said. "If they live over here then nine times outta ten their lil' asses is banging. If not," he shrugged, "call 'em casualties of war. Like the man said,

'It's a war out here and ain't nobody safe.'" He smiled wickedly and licked his lips as he brought his Uzi into play, gripping it with both hands. "Coast up, I'ma 'bout to eat some sea food."

"Fuck it," Nino shrugged, "Should have kept their baby asses inside."

He executed the headlights and slowed up the block. Bebop positioned himself in his seat and clutched his Uzi even tighter. He pointed the dusty black weapon out of the window and said, "What's popping, Blood!" the youths heads whipped around hearing the bellow. Bebop pulled the trigger just as something crashed into them from the rear. Bebop's Uzi spat recklessly out of the window as the Dodge fishtailed from the impact, crashing into an old Chrysler.

Nino blinked his eyes trying to fight the blood that was trying to seep into them. He was in a great deal of pain and could feel that his left hand was broken. He turned to Bebop and he was gritting his teeth in excruciation. His knee was busted and there was a nasty gash in his forehead. He looked out of the passenger side window and saw two men hopping out of a Nissan Pathfinder with a crash-bar. One was carrying something under his left arm while the other was clutching a gun of some sort. Seeing the man with the gun set off a panic alarm in Nino. He started up the car and threw it in reverse. He tried to back out but the fender was latched onto the bumper of the Chrysler.

"Y'all lil' niggaz get the fuck outta here!" one of the men shouted out to the two youths. The youngsters didn't waste any time riding off on the bike.

Boc! Boc!

The man toting the gun blew out both of the tires, startling Nino. He searched the floor for his Uzi but he couldn't find it. He then pulled on Bebop telling him that they had to get out of there. Nino climbed through the driver side window and fell out on his side, knocking the wind out of him. Bebop made to follow as fast as he could. He had grabbed hold of the window sill and was pulling himself out when someone snatched the passenger side door open. He looked back and saw the glow of a pair of evil eyes of a face partially blocked by long thick dreads. A large mitt reached out and grasped Bebop's ankle. With a strong yank, it pulled him from the car causing him to fall flat on his face on a street littered with broken glass. Before he knew it he was being pulled up by the back of his sweatshirt. The force was so great that Bebop felt like he was flying and he was a solid 240 pounds. Bebop was turned over and pressed up against the car. He clenched his jaws trying to thwart the pain in his knee. He momentarily forgot about his hurting once he heard three more gunshots…

Boc! Boc! Boc!

Nino hollered out in agony as slugs hit his back, severing his spinal cord and leaving him immobile. He dropped to his knees and fell on his belly in the middle of the street. Through the corner of his eye, Bebop saw the gun toting man approaching Nino with his gun extended before him. Bebop heard his homeboy whimpering. He closed his eyes as three more gunshots went off…

Boc! Boc! Boc!

Nino's whimpering stopped.

"Open your eyes." the voice rang loudly in Bebop's ears. He could feel the spittle hit his face. He slowly peeled open his eyes and stared into the ones before his. They were cold and plagued with murder. If he didn't know any better he would have sworn that it was a demon standing before him and not a man. He felt a hand wrap around his throat, slowing the air that flowed into his lungs. He looked down and saw his assailant's freehand reach into his waistline and snatch the world's biggest gun from it. He pressed the cannon into his forehead and barked, "When you get to hell…Tell'em O.G Paybacc sent chu!" Bebop's dome exploded, plastering chunks of gray brain fragments and blood on Paybacc's face. Paybacc released his victim's neck and allowed his corpse to fall to the street like a rag doll. Using the hand he held his banger in, Paybacc wiped the blood and chunks of brain from his face. He looked down at the lifeless body at his feet and rage mounted up in him again. "Punk ass, bitch ass, slob ass nigga!" he kicked the motionless form and popped two more slugs into its back. He tucked the heated, smoking gun into his waistline and reached for the gold urn that was on the roof of the car. "Come on, Domino, time to go." He took the gold urn into his large mitts, kissed it lovingly and tucking it under his right-arm.

"We're outro, Cuz. Let's bail." Chingo walked back to the Nissan Pathfinder, tucking his banger into his waistline. He hopped in behind the wheel. Paybacc placed the urn with Domino's ashes in it in the backseat and buckled the seatbelt around it as if it were a small child. Chingo watched him with a wrinkled forehead. He wondered if Paybacc was losing his mind. He talks to the urn as if it's Domino in the flesh and he takes it where ever he goes.

Chingo makes a right at the end of the block. Traveling up the main street he passed several oncoming police cruisers with their sirens blaring. Their cherry and berry lights shined through the windshield of the Pathfinder into his and

Paybacc's faces. The police had no idea that they had passed the vehicle carrying the men that had just wreaked havoc on the street they were heading to. Chingo smirked, finding the whole scenario ironic.

Gunshots went off in the distance. They weren't coming from just one designated area, but various parts of the city. The beef was cooking and there was an all-out war in the trenches. Armies of the Red and Blue republics were letting slugs fly over the loss of dead homies. As soon as Paybacc got the word that the homies had been massacred at the party, he gave the green-light on anything moving in red. He didn't care whether it was kids or old folks that got hit. He knew that he'd be breaking a code of old school morals by letting this slide, but reasoned that since the Bloods didn't give a fuck about murdering the little girl of one of the homies that no soul would be spared if they got in the way.

"It's hotter than fish grease out here," Chingo commented after hearing the ramped gun firing, "niggaz ain't gone be able to get a dime rock off in a minute."

"That's what it is then," Paybacc spoke, "this lil' nigga Booby don't respect nothing but murder, so we're gone have to turn it up on 'em. I was doing this gangsta shit when he was sucking on his momma's tit. He thinks he's doing something out here, but I'ma show 'em how a real G puts it down."

Shit, that's all I needed to hear. How in the fuck am I gonna convince this nigga to squash this beef so I can run these bands up? Chingo thought. I'm just gonna have to roll with the program until I come up with something.

$$$

C-Low stood in the full length mirror taking a look at the Air Jordan's 11 on his foot. He tilted his head from side to side, as he looked the basketball sneaker over. "What chu think, Choke?" he asked his homeboy, who was sitting on the bench texting someone on his Galaxy cell phone.

"Yeah, Cuz, them mothafuckaz are hard," he replied, not even looking up from his cell phone.

"Nigga, you're not even looking," C-Low barked, but continued to model his sneaker in the mirror. "Fuck it!" he turned to the shoe salesman. "Yo, let me get these in white, too." The shoe salesman nodded and went off to get the sneakers, leaving the two men alone in the store. C-Low sat down next to Choke and began to remove the sneaker from his foot.

"Man, it's like the world doesn't exist when you got that punk ass phone in your hand." C-Low told Choke.

"Are you jealous?" Choke asked, without taking his eyes from the cell phone.

C-Low sighed and blew air. "Whatever." He slid his foot into his own sneaker and placed the Air Jordan into its gray and black box, closing the lid. He looked up into the full length mirror and saw two gunmen wearing black bandanas over the lower halves of their faces, running into the shoe store with their bangers pointed at him. C-Low's eyes bugged and his mouth dropped open. He was petrified. He shot to his feet shouting, "Oh, shit!" Gunshots rang out as the gunmen ran upon their two unsuspecting targets…

Bloc! Bloc! Bloc! Boc! Boc! Bloc! Bloc! Bloc! Bloc! Boc! Boc!

Slugs slammed into C-Low and Choke's faces, bodies, arms and thighs. Specs of blood hit the sneakers lined up on the wall, as well as the clothes hanging from the ceiling. C-Low and Choke's bodies had what seemed like a thousand holes in them. They fell out on the floor on their backs and the gunmen ran upon them, continuing to fire. The gunmen looked up from where they stood over their victims and saw the shoe salesmen holding a box of Air Jordan's. He looked petrified. He wanted to make a run for it, but the menacing stares of the gunmen made him change his mind.

One of the gunmen pointed his banger at the shoe salesman's melon causing him to close his eyes tight. The gunman was just about to squeeze one off when his partner stopped him, by grabbing him by the wrist and lowering his hand.

"Fuck you doing, Blood? No civilians!" a feminine voice came from behind the black bandana of the gunman rocking a black beanie on her head. "Let's go, nigga!" she tapped her partner-in-crime and they fled the shoe store.

Scurrrrrrrrr!

The late model Acura Legend swung out of the shopping center parking lot recklessly. Cicero pulled the black bandana down from over his mouth and glanced out of the back window to make sure the police weren't on their tail.

"Yo, Maddy, gimmie your banger," Cicero pressed the button that opens the stash spot. He placed him and Maddy's bangers into the secret compartment along with their gloves and bandanas. He pressed the button again and the stash spot closed. He then took another glance out of the back window before relaxing back in his seat. "How long do you think we're gonna have to keep this shit up?"

"Until one of us kills Paybacc, or when the big homie calls it off," Maddy told him, "Booby's been on one since Gangsta got dropped, but I don't blame him. Them fiddles stole one of our Gs so they're supposed to feel it. Besides, if we don't keep dropping these niggaz then Booby's gonna cut off the drug line. There won't be any work for anybody, you heard'em. If we don't put in work then we don't eat."

And Booby's word was law.

FIVE

Ding!

The elevator sounded when it arrived on its designated floor. The doors divorced and Pavielle stepped out with the aid of his cane and Killa Dre by his side. A light skinned secretary with hair the color of red rose pedals and a dash of freckles on her cheeks, eyes bugged and mouth dropped wide open. Her face turned pale and she looked like she'd seen a ghost.

"What's popping, Naomi? How are you doing?" Pavielle asked with a hard face. "Is your punk ass daddy in his office?"

"Y…Yes," She nodded, looking scared as shit. Homegirl was too familiar with the gangsta's reputation in the streets. "But he's with a client of his."

"Oh, yeah?" Pavielle asked, not really giving a flying fuck. "Well, here's a buck," he smacked a dollar bill on her cluttered desk, "call someone that gives a fuck." He continued his stroll towards the double rosewood doors of Ziggy Blinkmen's office. Naomi, while keeping her eyes on the Pavielle and Killa Dre, discretely picked up her telephone and informed her father that Pavielle Hood was on the way to his office.

$$$

Ziggy Blinkmen was sitting behind his desk eating a Hero sandwich. A paper towel hung out of his collar to save his three hundred dollar shirt from any food droppings. Ziggy was grubboing on his sandwich and had just picked up his can of Pepsi Zero, when his telephone rung. He picked the phone

29

up and placed it to his ear. "Yello…" he said into the receiver as he began drinking the Pepsi.

"Dad, Mr. Hood and a young man are here to see you." Naomi informed Ziggy, causing him to spit the dark liquid all over the screen of his computer and key-board. He sat up in his executive chair and hung up the telephone. He sat the sandwich down on its wrapper and yanked the paper towel from his collar. He'd just pulled his desk drawer open and exposed a chrome .38 revolver with an ivory handle sitting inside, when he heard the footsteps growing closer as they met with the Italian marble floor outside of his office. He shot to his feet to lock the door when it came slamming into his face and knocking him on his back. His vision was blurred as he cupped his bleeding nose and mouth. His eyes lazily rose up from the floor and settled on the two hard-faces standing over him.

"Fuck is my mula, Ziggy?" Pavielle asked with a snarl.

"I, uh, I, uh," Ziggy fumbled with his words. Pavielle cocked his cane like a golf club and cracked Ziggy across the kneecap, drawing a howl of pain from him. He clutched his knee and clenched his teeth.

"Grrrrrrrrr," Ziggy grimaced and squared his jaws to combat the excruciation in his knee.

"Wrong answer; now, I'ma ask your conniving ass again…" Pavielle was cut short by Naomi's yelling.

"You guys better get out of here before I call the police." She said from her desk. With that said, Killa Dre whipped out his cannon and pointed it in Naomi's direction, causing her to stammer and tense. He advanced on her with a look in his eyes that dared her to pick up the telephone.

"Now why would you wanna go say some shit like that? Knowing damn well it has the potential to piss me off. Bring your ass over here!" Killa Dre yanked Naomi into him by her hair, drawing a yelp from her thin pink lip-stick lips. He pressed his joint into her spine and led her into Ziggy's office, where he planted her into the chair before the desk. "Move and I'ma send the top of your skull flying outta this room like Aladdin's carpet, you dig?" She nodded yes, as tears welled in her eyes; she swallowed the lump in her throat, fearfully.

"I gave you a million dollars of my money to buy the Bowen condos and you never purchased them. As a matter of fact, someone else swooped in and snatched the property right from under my nose. My fiancé told me she came up here to pick up the loot and you told her you'd already given it back to me. You told her this shit while I was in a coma. You thought I wasn't gonna pull through and you'd be free to run off with mine, didn't you? Well, hahahaha! The jokes on your mothafucking ass! I'm alive and I want my mothafucking paper!"

Pavielle grabbed Ziggy by his tie and pulled him to his feet. He reached his hand all the way to his back and brought it across Ziggy's face, loosening his back tooth. Ziggy staggered backwards and bumped into his desk. He spat blood on the floor and looked up at Pavielle, who was eye balling him evilly.

Wait! Wait!" Ziggy said, holding up his hand. "I can, I can get you your money."

Where is it? I want my shit right now!" he barked like a mad dig, spittle flying as he approached slowly, cane moving ahead in his victim's direction.

"I can get you a couple of grand right...Oof!" Ziggy's eyes bugged and his mouth dropped open. He clutched his stomach after Pavielle slammed the handle of his cane into it. The young kingpin then slammed the butt of the cane across his jaw and dropped him to the floor.

Pavielle threw his cane to the floor and whipped his .9mm automatic from the small of his back. "When I say I want my money now, I mean right goddamn now." He kneeled down to Ziggy and grabbed him by his jaw, tightly. He then pressed his banger to the accountant's temple. A wicked look surfaced on his face as he licked and bit down on his bottom lip. Naomi tried to rush to her father's aide but Killa Dre yanked her by the arm and pressed his joint further into her spine.

"What chu want on your tombstone?" Pavielle squeezed Ziggy's jaw so tight that his lips puckered up.

"Wait just a minute, Pavielle! Hear me out!" Ziggy pleaded.

"You better start talking...And fast." Pavielle commanded.

"I'm gonna level with ya," Ziggy began, "I don't have the money. I used it to pay off a gambling debt. I was in over my head with the mob."

"You know, Ziggy, if you're trying to convince me to let chu keep your life, you're doing a piss poor job right now."

"Let me finish," he begged, "I can take out some loans on a couple of properties of mine and give you the money. I just need a couple of weeks."

"Alright, Ziggy, I don't know why, but I'm going to take a chance on you. But I'm gonna need some collateral." Pavielle told him. "What cha got?"

"Cars, man! I'm talking top of the line luxury vehicles! I'm talking Ferrari, Benz, Porsche, Lamborghini; you name 'em I got 'em."

Pavielle took a moment to think it over. Coming to a conclusion, he removed the .9mm from Ziggy's dome and tucked it in the small of his back. He outstretched his hand and Ziggy hesitantly grasped it. Pavielle pulled him to his feet. He then adjusted his tie and smoothed the wrinkles out of his shirt. Ziggy was uncomfortable and visibly shaken by his touch. He closed his eyes and tried to control his trembling the entire time. Pavielle picked his cane up from the floor and looked into his eyes. "Alright, take me to these luxury cars that you were talking about."

"Just let me grab my jacket." Ziggy snatched his jacket off the back of the chair and picked his car-keys up from the desk. He fastened the buttons on his jacket and approached Naomi. He kissed her on the forehead and said, "I'll be right back, Pumpkin." He then headed out of the door with Pavielle and Killa Dre following closely behind.

$$$

Ziggy's head was heavy with sadness when he passed the pink slips to his most prized vehicles to Pavielle. Pavielle looked the pink slips over before slipping them into the breast-pocket of his shirt. Not giving a fuck about how Ziggy was feeling at the moment, he looked him in the eyes and said, "You've got two weeks to have the rest of my paper, Playboy. Two weeks. If you try to run I'll hunt chu down and I'll strap you to a chair. Then I'll cut your eyelids off so you'll have no choice but to watch as fifteen of my Y.Gs take turns fucking that pretty lil' daughter of yours up the ass. Once I figure you've had enough, I'll let my youngins take a crack at your wife. By then you'll be begging for me to kill you, then, and only then, will I put chu out of your misery. Do we understand one another?" Ziggy nodded. "Good, you have a nice day."

Pavielle hopped into the front passenger seat of Killa Dre's Charger and they rolled out of the circular driveway. With glassy eyes Ziggy watched as Pavielle's homeboys drove off behind him in the three whips he'd just signed over to him. First there was a Ferrari, followed by a Porsche 9/11 and then a CL 600 Mercedes Benz. Tears welled up in Ziggy's eyes and trickled down his cheeks. His head dropped and his chin touched his chest. He then wept like a five year old boy. He loved his cars just as much as he loved his children.

$$$

Killa Dre's cell phone rang. He looked to his cell and saw "Cicero" on the screen. He tapped the screen to answer, "What's up, Blood?" he asked, gripping the steering-wheel and guiding his sleek whip through the streets.

"Aye, ask the homie where we're taking these rides to." Cicero said.

Killa Dre looked to Pavielle.

"The homies wanna know where we're taking the cars."

Pavielle didn't hear Killa Dre. His eyes were focused out of the passenger side window. His attention was trained on two little black boys that were slap boxing in their front yard. The tallest one of the two was the lightest while the shorter one was the darkest. Though the shorter one's cheeks were red and he was getting the worse of it, he was still on his feet giving it his all. The taller one of the two was catching it and he eventually ended up falling on his back. That's when four teenagers stepped in and broke up the scrap. They ruffled the shortest one's head and gave him props. Seeing the two boys scrapping, Pavielle couldn't help but reflect on his current situation with Paybacc. Though he felt as if he was in a losing battle he was giving it his all and he would eventually be victorious.

"Yo, Big Homie," Killa Dre tapped Pavielle's arm and stole his attention. Pavielle turned around and threw his head back. "Where are we dropping these whips off?"

"Momma's house."

"We're heading back to the hood…G-Momma's house." Killa Dre said into his cell, which was mounted into the dashboard.

"Alright," Cicero responded.

Killa Dre ended the call and looked to Pavielle. "Yo, are you, all right?"

Pavielle nodded and replied. "I'm two hundred, all the time."

$$$

"What is the matter with your brother? I offer him my hand and he spits in it?" Black Jesus asked as he sat comfortably inside the backseat of his white on white Rolls Royce Phantom.

Gouch blew hard and shrugged. "Baby bro doesn't want to live in a dead man's shadow. He wants to establish himself as his own entity without the help of unc's friends and associates."

"In this business favors are exchanged regularly." Black Jesus told him. "At this level of the game there are certain relationships that are established to ensure that your run will be a long and fruitful one. The right associations could mean the difference between a thirty year stretch and a five year bid. It's because of these relationships that I haven't done time since '92."

"I see where you're coming from but baby bro is a hard head." Gouch stated. "He's not tryna hear me, you, his fiancé or anyone else."

"Alright, I can't make him take my help." Black Jesus said. "If he wants to handle this on his own, then so be it. But if the temperature rises out here you make sure get in touch with me…ASAP." He stared Gouch dead in his eyes and he gave him a nod before hopping out of the backseat of the Phantom. Gouch patted the roof of the Phantom and it drove off. He was about to step upon the curb when he caught something at the corner of his eye. He turned around and saw a line of luxury vehicles approaching. Seeing them he couldn't help but to get the feeling that a music video was about to be shot on his block. He knew better though, because nothing went down in the twenties without Booby's knowledge and/or say so.

Gouch's cell phone rang and he dipped his hand inside of his pocket. He pulled it out and saw his baby brother's name on the screen. He tapped the screen to answer the call and placed it to his ear.

"What's up?" he said into the cell.

"Pull open the gate, we're rolling up." Pavielle spoke before hanging up.

Gouch slipped his cell back inside of his pocket. He then unlocked the gate and pulled it open. He looked on as the line of luxury vehicles pulled inside of the driveway and drove into the backyard. Once he'd locked the gate back, Gouch started down the driveway and headed for the backyard. When he reached the backyard he found his baby brother, Killa Dre and a host of homies hopping out of the luxury vehicles.

"What's this?" Gouch asked of the luxury vehicles as he rubbed the hood of the Porsche 9/11.

"A deposit from Ziggy," Pavielle told him, looking back at all those expensive ass cars. "Homie didn't have that dough so I had to make 'em come up off something."

"Hey, fuck 'em," Gouch gave his baby brother dap.

"Fuck 'em." He replied. "Who was that I saw come through here?"

"B. J."

"Don't tell me, he insisted that I take him up on his offer, huh?" Gouch nodded. "Homeboy doesn't take no for an answer. Goddamn." He shook his head and pulled out his cell phone. He pulled up 'Black Jesus' and began punching in a message, his finger moving in swift motions cuing in bold letters. Gouch peeked over into the screen and saw the message: *FUCK OFF!* He then watched as Pavielle pressed 'send'.

"Fuck are you doing, Man? You tryna burn bridges with the plug?" Gouch frowned.

"I'm not wetting that spic, he's not going anywhere. I make too much paper for 'em." Pavielle informed him. "Besides, if he trips, fuck 'em, he can't be the only mothafucka out here with good coke." He was about to slip the cell phone back into his pocket when it rang and vibrated in his palm. A grin surfaced on his face once he saw that it was Black Jesus. He pressed 'ignore' and slipped the cell phone back into his pocket.

Pavielle noticed that Gouch was in his feelings from the expression on his face. He stepped to him and patted his cheek, gently. "You need to relax, Big Brother, you're too tense. You won't me to call up a skeeza? Get chu some lip service and some tail? Help you release some of that tension?"

Gouch straightened himself out.

"I'm Gucci."

"Great." Pavielle turned to Killa Dre and the rest of his men. "I'm in a good mood; let's say we all roll out to Shiznit tonight." All of the homeboys nodded and agreed that they should go out for a night on the town. "We're on then."

Pavielle moved to go inside of the house and Gouch grabbed him by his arm.

"Nigga, are you out of your skull? How are you gone go to a titty bar when you got an army of Head Bustas gunning at chu."

Pavielle yanked his arm back and said, "Easy, bosses do what they want and workers do what they are told." He looked him up and down like he wasn't shit.

Gouch stared daggers at Pavielle's back as he headed into the house.

$$$

A smirk emerged on Black Jesus' face as he read over the text he'd been sent by Pavielle. He caressed the screen of his cell phone with his thumb as he stared down at the display, casually taking pulls from his Cuban cigar.

"What's up?" Bullet threw his head back as he peeled an orange.

"Take a look." Black Jesus passed him the cell phone. He lay back taking pulls from the cigar as he watched him read over Pavielle's text.

Bullet raised an eyebrow and shook his head. He passed the cell phone back to Black Jesus.

"That's some disrespectful shit, Bro; Booby's talking to you as if you're one of his pinche workers." Bullet spoke his mind.

Black Jesus took the cell phone and tucked it back inside of his light grey Armani suit. "Booby has gotten beside himself. I know his uncle's death has taken a toll on him, so I've been trying to bear with him, but there is only so much that I am willing to take." He sighed and took a drag from his cigar. The white smoke swirled and whipped around his person. It gave you the illusion that a magician had waved his magic wand and made him appear there on the spot.

"Killa and the boy Gouch are cool, but it seems to be Booby that has forgotten that you're that spic and that you can have him squashed like the cockroach that he is." Bullet spoke on it. "One phone call could have his skinny black ass ripped off of the map. Matter of fact, you want me to put a call into Tito and make that happen?"

Black Jesus shook his head no.

"Charles would turn over in his grave if he knew that his dearest amigo had his nephew's wig pushed back." Black Jesus told him. "No. I won't get at him through violence. There's three ways to get at a man like Booby. And that's by fucking with his pride, his woman, or his money."

"True." Bullet nodded.

"Take a wild guess of which one I'm going to fuck with?"

Black Jesus smiled wickedly and partook in his cigar.

SIX

Vida pushed the Dodge Magnum through traffic. Voodoo played the passenger seat while G-thang and Dip resided in the backseat. Voodoo's face was made up to cover her tattoos and her hair was dyed blonde and braided into cornrows. G-thang's dome was bald and shiny. He looked like a black Mr. Clean with his clean shaven face. Dip wore a shaved head and a thin mustache. The collective looked nothing like they once did. It was nearly impossible for their mothers to recognize them.

The stereo was on a Spanish radio station and a Latino crooner was singing his heart out as his band serenaded him. The volume was at a medium level but no one was actually listening to the music. Each individual was swamped in his or her own thoughts. They wondered what their lives would be like after they were whisked away to the other side of the world, neither of them had been out of their hood, save for Los Vegas. They breathed, ate, and shat in the ghettos of South Central, Los Angeles. They were products of their environments and didn't see anything past their hood, so getting adjusted to a new land was going to take some time.

"Yo, Vida, you missed the block we were supposed to turn on." G-thang said from the backseat where he took a 40 oz of Olde English to the head.

"For real?" Vida asked.

"Unh huh," G-thang nodded after taking the 40 oz from his lips and wiping his mouth with the back of his hand.

"Yeah, Babe, you missed it, see?" Voodoo pointed to the street they'd passed by on the MapQuest print out.

"Damn." Vida said.

"It's cool, Baby Girl, bust a bitch." G-thang passed the 40oz to Dip. Dip grasped the bottle and turned it up, guzzling it as if he was the thirstiest man on the earth. G-thang looked at him sideway. He could still tell that the murder of the little girl was fucking with his mental and he was trying to kill any feelings he had about it.

"You see The Ones?" Vida asked as she gripped the steering-wheel, making to turn.

G-thang looked around and didn't see the police in sight. He settled back in his seat and said, "Nah, you good, Sis, gone bust it."

Vida executed the U-turn successfully. She got about a half a block away from the street she had missed her turn on when she heard the familiar chirp of a police siren. That sound made Voodoo, G-thang and Dip tense and their hearts race. Vida looked into the rearview mirror and saw a police officer on a motorcycle.

"Damn, G, I thought you said she was good?" Voodoo frowned.

"Shit she was. That mothafucka came outta nowhere." G-thang screwed the cap on the 40 oz and sat it on the floor between his legs. "Everybody play it cool, act natural; this cracka will probably just hit us with a ticket and let us be on our way."

"Pull over, Babe," Voodoo told Vida. She saw that her lover was nervous. "You got this, just relax. Pull right here." She pointed to a shaded part of the street that trees hung over. Vida did as she was told. Voodoo rubbed her thigh as she tried to gather her wits. Discreetly, she slipped her joint off of her waistline and hid it under her long white T-shirt, clicking the safety off of it. She then looked up into the rearview mirror. She locked eyes with G-thang and gave him a nod. He gave one back letting her know that he had his joint out as well. He had his gripped firmly beside his leg.

"Be ready in case this shit goes South, Dip." G-thang whispered.

Dip nodded. He was under the influence of the cheap liquor but the threat of being locked up was quickly sobering him up. He adjusted his joint on his waistline where he could quickly grab it if shit got funky.

"Shhhhh," Voodoo hushed them, seeing the officer in the rear view mirror. "Here he comes."

The police officer approached the Magnum, shining his flashlight around in the backseat into G-thang and Dip's faces. They narrowed their eyes and frowned when the intense beam came across their faces. The officer shined his light at G-thang's feet and saw the 40 oz of Olde English. His nose twitched as he sniffed the air. Seeing this, Voodoo mouthed to herself "fuck". She knew he had caught a whiff of the Kush that they'd blown on the way over.

"Is there a problem, Officer?" Vida asked, smiling.

"Step out of the car, all of you." The officer ordered.

"Wait a minute; you aren't going to ask for my L's or my registration?" Vida wanted to know.

"Ma'am, I'm not going to tell you all again." The officer raised his voice. "Get out of the car now!"

Voodoo looked up into the rearview mirror into G-thang's eyes. He gave a nod and brought his joint into play. The officer was so busy going back and forth with Vida that he didn't even notice that he had a banger pointed at his chest. G-thang's finger brushed against the trigger.

Boom!

An Avalanche truck crashed into the officer's motorcycle sending it tumbling forth, coming apart. The officer dove out of the way of the hurling motorcycle narrowly missing it. G-thang pulled his joint back inside. The officer got to his feet, looking into the windshield of the Avalanche truck. A young Mexican man was behind the wheel. His eyes were red and glazed over. He looked around like he didn't know what just happened. The officer could tell that he was drunk.

"Fucking asshole," The officer said under his breath. He looked to Vida and said. "Are you OK to drive?" she nodded yes. "Go ahead and get out of here."

As the officer limped towards the Avalanche truck, Vida fired up the Magnum and pulled off. Everyone else sighed with relief. It was a close call but now they were scot-free.

"Big G looking out for us tonight," Voodoo spoke of God Almighty.

"Straight up," G-thang cracked a smile, "I thought I was gone have to soak that pig's uniform." He picked up the 40 oz from between his legs and twisted off the cap. He tilted it to take a swig and caught Dip at the corner of his eye. He looked and Dip was staring out of the window. He could only see the side of his face but he could tell that he was troubled.

G-thang nudged Dip and he looked to him. "Are you all right, Blood?"

"I'm A1, Duse Owe." Dip replied then continued to stare out of the window.

G-thang watched Dip for a time before taking a swig of his liquor. He knew that Dip was far from OK, but he wasn't going to press him to talk. He'd leave him to his thoughts for the time being. He figured that once they'd gotten relocated and he'd gotten himself a piece of ass that he'd start to feel better. He knew that his homeboy would be all right. All he needed was some tail, a drink and a fat ass blunt and then he'd be back to his normal self.

SEVEN

A cherry red H2 Hummer pulled up outside of club Shiznit. Its glossy paint and chrome 28 inch rims shined under the illumination of the street lights. The Hummer looked like it had just been driven off the showroom floor. Any onlookers would have thought its owner had just purchased the vehicle mere seconds ago. The only thing that would have given it away was that there weren't any tags in the windshield.

Three more exotic vehicles pulled up behind the Hummer. There was a canary yellow Lamborghini, a midnight blue BMW 745 and a egg shell white X5. Pavielle threw the passenger side door of the Hummer open and jumped down onto the sidewalk. He adjusted his icy gold pinky ring and surveyed his surroundings, his eyes concealed by Louie Vuitton shades.

He was fresh to death in a Louie Vuitton vest and matching Louie Vuitton sneakers.

While Pavielle stood his ground taking in his surroundings, the rest of his entourage assembled behind him. He stepped in motion towards the entrance of the gentlemen's club with his crew bringing up the rear. The collective moved in on the entrance of the gentlemen's club where a bald headed man stood. He had a peanut shaped head and the body of a young Schwarzenegger. He was dressed in a black T-shirt and a black blazer that was too short at the sleeves and struggling to contain his mass.

Pavielle stopped dead smack in front of the peanut head bouncer. He came to his chin so he had to look up at him. He reached into his pocket and pulled out a wad of money that was secured by a rubber-band. The wad was so big that he had trouble pulling it out of his jeans. Pavielle popped the rubber-band and shifted through the dead white men, looking up at the peanut head bouncer.

"We're in this thang; how much for me and my set, Boss Dawg?" he asked like money was nothing to him, which it wasn't.

"Nuh unh," Peanut head shook his bald dome no. "There's no way I'm letting y'all rowdy asses in here. The last time we had to shut this bitch down early."

"That shit wasn't our fault, Fam, we were up in here tryna have a good time. It was old boy who started that ruckus." Pavielle told him the truth.

"Straight up," Gouch draped his arm over Killa Dre's shoulders. "Homeboy spilled champagne in our Y.G's dreads on purpose, it was a must he got that work. You Griff me?"

"Look, Boss, I'ma lay this stack on you and pay whatever it is to get my niggaz in here tonight." Pavielle counted out a G-stack and held it out towards the peanut head bouncer.

The peanut head bouncer looked down at the G-stack and blew hard, massaging his chin. The money was sweet and he wanted to take it. But his boss warned him that if he let Pavielle and his crew in next time and some shit popped off that his big ass was getting fired. With bills up the yin yang and child support for two kids he couldn't afford to lose his job.

"Nah, Man!" the peanut head bouncer shook his head. "I can't fuck with chu. It's my ass if shit go south up in there."

Pavielle counted out another grand and held it out towards the bouncer. "Here. take these two stacks and gone let us through."

"Nah, Bruh, I'm not fucking with y'all." The peanut head bouncer stood his ground.

"Let me holla at chu," Pavielle motioned the bouncer over to the side away from the ears of his entourage. Once Pavielle and the bouncer were off to the side alone, he addressed him in a calm voice, staring into his eyes. "Check this out, G," he thumbed his nose, "Either you let us in here tonight, or we're gone clap this shit up before we leave and each and every night y'all open. Imagine how business will plummet then. These tricks ain't gone wanna come here to toss they dollars when they gotta worry about catching a hot one." The bouncer blew hard and massaged the bridge of his nose, contemplating. "Make this easy on the both of us: take this lil' change and let me and my boys in. We're just here to have a good time. That's all. We don't want any trouble."

Pavielle stuck the two G-stacks inside of the peanut head bouncer's blazer and patted it. He then peeled off a few C-notes for the admission fees of his homeboys. He extended his jeweled hand and the bouncer plucked the bills from his mitt.

"Y'all not packing are y'all? If so leave them shits outside, Man."

"My dude, now you know how I roll." Pavielle looked at him as if he knew better. "I'm not treading through that ho without them thangs. The last time I went in naked one of my dudes caught a hot one in the shoulder. Ain't no way I'm stepping through that door without a piece."

"Alright, but don't start no shit in here."

"Like I told you, we're just here to have a good time. We don't want any trouble." Pavielle assured him.

The bouncer threw his head towards the club entrance and walked off with Pavielle following behind. He unhooked the velvet rope and stepped aside, allowing the young kingpin and his niggaz inside.

As soon as Pavielle and his entourage crossed the threshold into Club Shiznit, their ears were assaulted by Bel Biv Devoe's "Poison". There were women walking around scantily clad or completely naked. An Amazon of a waitress waltz right passed Pavielle carrying drinks on a tray. Her water melon sized breasts and enormous ass jumped slightly with every step she took. She looked Pavielle in the eyes and he noticed that she was wearing yellow cat eye contacts. Her long wet tongue emerged from between her blue lipstick covered lips and licked her top lip. She smirked and continued past Pavielle, dragging a manicured nail across his chin.

The hoots, hollers and cheers of men drew Pavielle's attention to the stage. There he found a rather geeky looking man in glasses and a suit jacket sitting in a chair. He wore red heart printed boxers and his slacks were around his ankles. A slim chick with long wavy hair and a healthy ass grinded on the lap of the geeky man sensually. He licked his lips and bit down on his bottom lip seeing his boner wedged between her butt cheeks. The slim chick looked over her shoulder and into his eyes, licking her tongue at him like a serpent. Her hands gripped his thighs as she slid her rump up and down the protrusion in his boxers. From the expression on the geeky man's face it was obvious that he'd ejaculated in his underwear. After a job well done, the slim chick jumped to her blue stiletto pumps and pulled her blue G-string over the geeky man's head. She then kissed her fingers and placed them to his lips.

"Everybody give a hand for Poison!" The DJ spoke into the microphone.

The audience rose to their feet applauding and whistling, giving the slim chick praise. She threw her head back and her hands in the air. She bent at the waist to give a bow.

Boom!

Boom!

Frooooosh!

Fire erupted from both sides of the black marble stage and the reddish orange flames licked the air. The slim chick kissed her palm and blew the crowd a kiss before strutting backstage, her butt cheeks jiggling with every step she took.

"Come on, Baby Bro." Gouch nudged Pavielle and snapped him out of his trance. He looked around and saw that he and his entourage were being lead to the V.I.P section.

Pavielle and his niggaz were doing it up in Shiznit. They'd gotten loaded off of Loud and champagne. In fact, their table had amassed so many bottles of Ace of Spades that you would have thought that they were gathering them to drop off at a recycling center. The area of the V.I.P section that they chilled in was heavy with weed and nicotine smoke; so much that they could barely be made out through it. Pavielle made sure all of his niggaz were taken care of. Each man got a lady or two of his choosing, all on the boss man's dime. Gouch and Killa Dre were the only ones out of the clique that didn't allow themselves' to get too relaxed. Pavielle had insisted that they take up time with a couple of girls but they declined. They opted to stick by Pavielle's side like Velcro, making sure that he was all right.

White smoke wafted around Pavielle as he took pulls from a blunt. He was high out of his mind and his eyes were narrowed into slits, making him look like a black Richard Gere. He was sunk in the plush black leather sofa watching the scenery of the gentlemen's club while consuming some of the finest marijuana Cali had to offer. He'd forgotten his pain killers at home. But it wasn't like he needed them anyway. All of the drugs he'd partaken that night made him impervious to the soreness of his gunshot wounds. That night he'd popped two X pills, blew three blunts and bodied two bottles of champagne. It was safe to say that he was shit faced and as horny as a jack rabbit. He'd had pussy thrown at him all night but his love and loyalty to Vayda was ho proof. He hadn't fucked around since he'd proposed to her. He couldn't front though, seeing all the tits and ass frolicking about made it hard to ignore the calling in his loins. The alcohol and drugs he'd consumed didn't help either.

Figuring that he should call it a night before his dick got him in any extra-curricular activities, Pavielle mashed the ember of his blunt out in the ashtray and shot to his feet. He gave a quick scan of the club and saw his niggaz scattered throughout the floor, still turning up. He tucked what was left of his blunt behind his ear and cupped his hand around his mouth. He called out to Gouch who was guarding the velvet rope outside of the V.I.P section.

"Gucci," Pavielle called out. "Assemble the troops."

Gouch gave his baby brother a nod. He said something into Killa Dre's ear before heading off to gather the homies.

Pavielle guessed that he'd told him to hold it down until he'd gathered every one.

"You about to take it in, Boo?" a sexy voice came from behind Pavielle.

He looked to his right and found the chick that had performed on stage earlier that night. She'd kept him company in the beginning of the night, but had to leave to snatch the few dollars the small fish were throwing since Pavielle wasn't big on tricking. They'd chopped it up for a while and had enjoyed one another's conversation. Pavielle thought she was a pretty cool chick. She was laidback, funny, intelligent and sexy as hell. He'd found himself strangely drawn to her. He wanted so badly to rip that blue G-string from off her and give her a taste of his long stroke, but the G in him kept him at bay. He wasn't about to jump out of the window behind some broad he'd just met. He had way too much player in him for that.

"Yeah, we're about to eighty six."

"Awww," She pouted, making a sad face like a baby. "Aren't chu gonna gimmie a goodbye kiss?" she tapped her cheek with a French tip finger nail.

Pavielle looked beyond the velvet rope where his crew had assembled and signaled for them to give him a minute. He approached the blue lipstick, blue G-string rocking stripper known as Poison. A smile was stretched across her face. It really played up the diamond studs in her dimples. Pavielle leant closer to give her a peck on the cheek and she turned her head, making his lips mash against her pillow soft lips. The young kingpin smirked while she smiled and giggled.

"You think you're slick, huh?" he asked.

"I am...When I'm wet." She quipped, smiling.

"That's what's up."

"Why don't chu shoot me your contact, Sweetie?"

"You know I gotta fiancé, right?"

"And? You ain't saying nothing."

"Oh, it's like that?"

"Straight up," She stated sincerely. She picked up an ink pen from the tray and passed it to him. She then pulled out her left breast and showed him where to sign. She bit down on her bottom lip and eyed him seductively. Once Pavielle finished inking his digits on her breast, he handed her back her ink pen. She took his cell phone and programmed her number into it before giving it back.

"Alright, Jamie," he addressed her by the name she'd programmed her number under in his cell. "I'll holla at chu."

"OK then, Boo." she kissed her fingers and touched them to his lips. She sashayed off throwing a little something more in her walk, making that scrumptious ass of hers bounce like a six four Impala with switches in a throwback Dr. Dre music video.

"Lord have mercy." Pavielle shook his head and bit down on his bottom lip.

Pavielle and his entourage emerged from Club Shiznit and confiscated their vehicles. Once he dropped a healthy tip to the valet, the Hummer pulled away from the scene. Followed by the midnight blue BMW 745, the canary yellow Lamborghini and the egg shell white X5. Paybacc stepped onto the curb and lit up a cigarette, blowing smoke from his nostrils. He watched the back lights of the X5 until they disappeared into the night.

EIGHT

Pavielle opened the door of his home and staggered inside, gripping a bottle of Ace of Spade by the neck. He could barely walk he was so faded but that didn't stop him from trying. He moved forth and ended up bumping into an end table and knocking over a vase. The vase hit the marble floor and exploded into pieces.

"Ah, fuck me!" Pavielle cursed, looking at the broken pieces of vase at his feet. He sat the bottle of Ace of Spades on the end table and bent down to his knees. He went about the task of trying to pick up the broken pieces and ended up slicing his hand. He winced and grabbed his wrist, staring down at his palm. There was a bloody gash there that rolled down the crevasses of his palm and dripped on the floor. Pavielle looked from the small splatters of blood on the floor and back to his palm before balling it closed into a fist. Hearing soft footfalls, he looked up and saw Vayda coming down the staircase with a pretty chrome thang in her grasp. It was a .357 revolver with a pearl handle. He'd given it to her to hold the house down while he was away. The homies that he kept outside the door was the first line of defense while she was the last.

"It' alright, V, it's me." Pavielle told her as he got to his feet, cradling his wounded hand.

Vayda dropped the .357 into the pocket of her house coat and engaged her fiancé. Concern came over her face once she'd saw the droplets of blood at his feet.

"What happened?" she asked, taking a look at his hand.

"I sliced my hand tryna pick up these broken pieces of vase." He told her.

"I see." She said. "You're probably gonna need stitches." She looked up into his eyes and saw that they were red and glassy. His legs were barely holding him up. She could tell that he was drunk. She threw his arm over her shoulders and headed towards the staircase.

"Where are we going?" Pavielle asked.

"The bathroom, I'm gonna patch that hand up." Vayda told him.

$$$

Vayda sat Pavielle down on the edge of the tub and retrieved the first aid kit from under the cabinet. She kneeled down to the tiled floor and went about the task of cleaning and dressing up Pavielle's wound. While she was wrapping Pavielle hand in an Ace-Bandage she looked up at him and saw his chin touching his chest and his eyes closed. From the way he was breathing she could tell that he was asleep. She smirked and finished bandaging his hand. She kissed his hand and slowly rose to her feet. Her eyes narrowed into slits when she saw something on the collar of his shirt. She peered closely and saw that it was a blue lipstick imprint there.

Vayda's face melted into a scowl and her eyes ignited. She clenched her teeth so tight that her jawbones pulsated.

Smack!

When Vayda's palm went across Pavielle's face, it woke him up as well as stung his cheek. Before he could gather his wits her palm was coming across his face a second time. This made him look alive and grab her about the wrists before she could strike him again. Pavielle frowned and forced Vayda up against the glass wall of the shower.

"Fuck is wrong with you, Girl?" Pavielle snarled.

"What hole you done ran your dick up in tonight?" Vayda spat with a throat poisoned with venom.

"What the hell are you talking about?"

"The lipstick on the collar of your shirt!"

Pavielle released Vayda's left wrist and pinched his collar, bringing it closer so that he could see it. Seeing the blue lipstick there he quickly formed an excuse for it, but as he parted his lips to speak he was being punched in the jaw. The blow whipped his head around and he felt it in his teeth, but it wasn't enough to get him off of her. He was on fire now. He pulled Vayda from the wall and twisted her arm behind her back, forcing her up against the shower's glass wall. Her face winced in pain as he pulled her arm upwards near the back of her head. Tears cascaded down her cheeks and over her lips. She was more hurt from her lover's disloyalty than the hurting he was putting on her. Pavielle snatched the .357 from Vayda's house coat pocket and placed it to the back of her head.

"Calm your ass down, I didn't fuck nobody!" Pavielle barked, spittle flying from his lips. "I gotta couple lap dances at the club, but I didn't run up in any of them hoes! I don't know what kind of disease them bitches probably got!"

"You're a fucking liar, I hate cho ass! Ohhh! I swear to God!" she swore and shuddered, breaking down crying.

Pavielle took the .357 from the back of Vayda's dome and released her arm. She balled up into a fetal position on the floor and bawled.

"That's on my momma, my daddy, G-momma and all my dead homie's graves I didn't touch any of them girls at that club. I wouldn't do you like that. But now I wish I would have…Shit, I got the headache for it anyway." Pavielle opened the chamber of the .357 and dumped the bullets out into his palm. He then stuffed the bullets into his pocket and dropped the .357 on the floor beside Vayda.

Pavielle left Vayda in the bathroom looking stupid.

$$$

Smack!

Smack!

Smack!

Her buttocks sounded each time his bare hips slammed into them and caused ripples to travel up her ass. She was bent over with her hands gripping the ledge of the dresser and the heels of her pumps stabbed into the flat carpet of the cheap motel room. Her face was twisted into a mask of pleasure. She screamed and watched him fuck her from the back like a raging maniac, as he held her Brazilian 22 inch hair back in a tight grasp. She stared into Pavielle's eyes through the reflection of the mirror as he punished her with back shots. Her pussy farted as his schlong crashed in and out of her womb unmercifully. His eyes projected anger and he gritted his teeth. He let go of her hair and pulled her sweaty body against his, wrapping his hand around her throat choking her. A smile stretched across her face and she licked her lips. She tried to kiss him but he turned his head, wrapping his other hand around her throat. He rammed into her hard. At this point he wasn't trying to appease her; he was trying to hurt her. She ate it up though; loving every second of it.

"Yes, Baby, that's how I like it. Fuck me!" she egged him on, estacy written all over her face. "Fuck my brains out; I've been a naughty girl!"

"You like this shit?" he asked, veins bulging at his temples and neck. "You like a nigga to fuck your ass like a dirty lil' slut, huh?"

"Yes! Yes! Yes!" she hollered, eyes rolling to their whites. "Take it! Take it! It's yours! Oh God…" she trailed off and went hoarse as he continued to give it to her raw and uncut like a stud in a hardcore porn flick.

Tiring of that position, he backed out of her and smacked her right ass cheek where her name was in Japanese letters going straight down.

"Climb up on the bed on your hands and knees!" he ordered. He watched her do as he'd instructed while taking a 5th of Hennessy to the dome. He removed his jeans from around his ankles and removed his Polo boxer briefs. He would have been butt ass naked if it weren't for his socks. He hopped upon the bed and stood over her waddling ass. Using his right hand, he pressed his dick downward and slowly kneeled, easing his black steel into the wet interior of her Fuck Tunnel. She licked her chops and hissed like a feral cat as each inch of his Bitch Pleaser crept inside of her sopping moisture. She bit down on her bottom lip and looked over her shoulder, watching him as he gain access to the Paradise between her legs.

Once he was half way inside of her, he gripped her shoulders and brought his black pole down in a slope. He laid into her hard and fast. He drilled his Bitch Pleaser into her creamy opening from its head all the way down to its balls. He gave her the whole thang. Not giving a mad ass fuck if she could handle it all. Each time he threw himself into her heart shaped ass, beads of sweat flew from his face and body and onto her back. The whole episode was intense. He could feel his shaft quickly filling with semen. Veins bulged in his arms, neck and forehead. His face displayed the pressure that had built up in his loins and was ready to be unleashed. Finally, he busted off, slamming his Fuck Stick inside of her three last times and holding the last one there while he took a breather. Once he'd gathered his wits, he slowly pulled his limp schlong from out of her and saw that the condom had broken. The beige rubber was still around his shaft but his dick head was exposed at the tip.

"Shit!" Pavielle cursed, pulling the ruined latex from his endowment.

"Don't worry about it, Baby, I'm on the shot." Poison informed him.

"That's what's up." He tossed the ruined condom into the trash basket and collapsed on the bed, breathing hard.

"Wifey must have really pissed you off." Poison said with her elbow planted into the bed and the side of her face resting in her palm.

"What gave you that idea?"

"Nigga, you was literally tryna kill this pussy."

"All of that freak shit you were popping on the way over here and you can't handle the dick?"

"Oh, I can handle it, Baby, I'ma big girl." She capped as she massaged his length and got it back harder than ever. "Tell your lil freak bitch what wifey did so I can make it all better."

"Fuck are you my psychologist?" Pavielle asked annoyed. "Shut up and suck my cock!" he pushed her head down and her mouth enveloped his manhood. He placed his hands behind his head and closed his eyes, allowing her mouth to take him to a place you could only visit with a passport. The feeling of Poison's wet tongue and the warmth of her mouth zapped Pavielle to Miami. He saw himself emerging from out of a pool dripping wet and the sun shining upon his hind and warming his body. The thought brought a smile to his face and five minutes later he was melting inside of her mouth.

$$$

Pavielle awoke the next morning feeling the aches of his wounds. His brow furrowed from the pain as his eyes tried to adjust to the sunlight. He checked his surroundings and found Poison hugging his waist fast asleep. Her drool had pooled around her mouth and had dried on his stomach. She smacked her lips and rubbed her nose, then started back snoring. Pavielle looked beyond her head and saw his dick still in a condom. He glanced at his Presidential Rolex and saw that it was two o'clock in the afternoon. He snatched his cell phone off of the nightstand. He had fifteen missed calls and ten of them were from Vayda. Fuck! He silently cursed to himself. He knew he was going to get an earful when he got back home.

Smack!

"Ouch!" Poison's head shot up and she looked at Pavielle like he was crazy, holding her stinging thigh. "Fuck is wrong with you, Nigga?"

"Get cho ass up, it's time for me to go." Pavielle pulled the condom from off of his cock and dropped it into the wastebasket. He went to sit up and pain shot through his torso, causing him to clench his jaws tightly, exposing the muscles in them. It became apparent to him that all of the drugs and alcohol from last night had worn off. He didn't have any pain killers on him so liquor would have to do. He looked to the dresser and saw the 5th of Hennessy sitting there.

"Toss me that Hen Dog." He told Poison as she sauntered her naked body around the bed. She snatched the bottle of Hennessy from off of the dresser and tossed it to Pavielle. He cracked the seal and guzzled the dark liquor, watching her butt cheeks dance all of the way to the bathroom. He wanted so badly to bust that pussy wide open again, but his wounds were wreaking havoc on him and he had to get home to his fiancé.

Pavielle got dressed and dropped a few dollars on the nightstand for Poison a cab before heading for the door. The door slammed and Poison came darting out of the bathroom with a towel wrapped around her. She looked to the dead men Pavielle had dropped on the nightstand to the door.

"Damn." Poison cursed and headed back into the bathroom. She was hoping to get some more dick before he left.

$$$

Pavielle came through the door calling out Vayda's name. When he didn't get a response he headed up to their master bedroom. He pulled open the nightstand drawer and picked up his bottle of pain killers, heading into the bathroom where he turned on the golden faucet. He cupped his hand under the flowing water. Next, he threw back the two tiny pills and then the water behind it. Afterwards, he splashed water on his face and took a deep breath. He grabbed a towel and began patting his face dry. When he looked up he saw Vayda in the doorway breast feeding their baby boy and giving him the evil eye. If looks could kill Pavielle would be riddled with holes and lying in a pool of blood. After a stare down that seemed like a century, the future Mrs. Hood left the doorway and walked out of the bedroom.

"Fuck it, it is what it is." Pavielle went back to patting his face dry.

NINE

A couple of nights later

Pavielle climbed the steps with his fingers wrapped around a glass of Cognac, taking sips along the way. His eyes were glassy and the odor seeping from his pores was repugnant. He was shit faced and high as a satellite. Pavielle peeked inside of the master bedroom, but Vayda wasn't there so he headed into Nasheed's bedroom. He turned the corner into the bedroom just in time to see her laying the little guy inside of his crib. He stood in the doorway watching as Vayda leant over and kissed their son on the side of the head. Pavielle smirked seeing this display of affection. Vayda was startled when she turned around and saw Pavielle standing in the doorway. She didn't hear him enter the bedroom, nor could she feel his presence.

"Hey, I didn't see you standing there." Vayda said, approaching. "When did you get in?"

"Just now," Pavielle answered. He leant forward to kiss her and she placed her hand on his chest, stopping him. Pavielle frowned and she left the bedroom with him on her heels. "Hold up, I know you aren't still tripping?" he asked, grabbing a hold of Vayda's arm as she crossed the threshold into their master bedroom. She turned around to face him, looking him directly in the eyes.

"I don't know who you are anymore." She twisted up her facem looking him up and down.

"I told you I'm not fucking around, I was straight up." He lied.

"You really expect me to believe that shit? I was born at night, not last night." Vayda shot back. "You staggered in here 3-4 o' clock in the morning, with lipstick on your collar and expect me to believe you aren't dicking down the next bitch? How would it look to you if I came home with some nigga'z semen on my dress? How would you react then?" she placed her hand on her hip and shifted her weight to the other leg. "Oh, yeah, and let's not forget you coming in late ass hell a couple of nights ago. Is that how we're doing it now, Pavy? Huh? Is there some new rules you made up that I don't know about?"

"Nah, and if you ever tried to play me, I'd be calling my brother to help me bury the body. Don't front like you don't know how I give it up." He took a sip of Cognac. Mad dogging her ass over the rim of the glass.

"See, that's what I don't understand about chu men." Vayda began. "You figure you can fuck with any and every bitch you damn well please. But as soon as we step out you wanna Black Ball us. Fuck is that about?"

"I hear all of that shit chu popping, but don't none of it apply to me." Pavielle told her. "I've been faithful since day-one. I've only got eyes for you."

"Yeahhhh," she shot him a look that said *'I know you don't expect me to believe that?'* "Lie to daddy, tell momma the truth."

"Fuck is that supposed to mean?" he asked defensively.

"It means that I don't believe your ass, you're gonna have to come again." She moved her neck how Ghetto Girls do when they're angry and popping more shit than a little bit.

"You know what, fuck it then!" he fired back. "I'm not finna do tricks and jump through flaming hoops to prove nothing to your ass! Fuck I look like?"

"Shhhh," Vayda placed a finger to her lips. "Lower your voice, you're gonna wake the baby."

Pavielle went on as if he didn't hear her.

"I can't believe you dropped this shit on me after the year I've had? Any other man would have crumbled like a Fortune Cookie if he had to cope with what I have." He took another sip of Cognac and it seemed to fuel his heated rant. "This nigga Paybacc running around out here gunning up my people, putting the game in a twist and fucking up my money. But he still can't stop me, 'cause I'm still getting mine. I'm getting this paper and in time I'ma get his faggot ass, too."

"Yeah, if he doesn't get you first," she said under her breath.

"What chu say? I couldn't hear you?" his face balled up.

"Nothing," She replied, as she sat at the vanity and began pinning up her hair.

"Nah, you said something, go ahead and repeat it, with your red ass." He came to stand behind her.

Vayda turned around in her chair. "I said, 'if he doesn't get you first.'"

Pavielle was taken aback; he licked the inside of his jaw and looked at Vayda sideways. "You'd love for that to happen, wouldn't chu? That way you could run off with my money; that's just like a trifling whore. I should have known better, you can't turn a ho into a house wife!" he lifted the glass to his lips to take a sip and she smacked the glass from his hand. The glass hurled across the bedroom and exploded into the wall, sending broken pieces everywhere. The dark liquid it contained ran down the wall and absorbed into the cream mink carpet.

Pavielle was as mad as a hornet. His glassy eyes had turned red and veins formed in his forehead and neck. His nostrils flared and he breathed heavily. Vayda was scared now, but it was too late. She'd laid down the gauntlet. Pavielle grabbed her about the neck and slammed her up against the wall, denting a small hole in it. He clenched his jaws and squeezed her windpipe, putting a strain on the oxygen that passed through it. She squirmed under his powerful grip, whipping her head back and forth, struggling to breathe. Her eyes turned glassy and red, while her face became the color of a rose pedal. She gagged and tried to knee Pavielle in the balls, but he stuck his legs between her own. He then brought his other hand into play and applied pressure with both of his mitts.

"You want to disrespect me in my house, Bitch?!" his eyes bursted into flames. "You must think I'm one of those niggaz you used to turn tricks with! Well, I'm not the one! You hear me?" he shook her by the neck violently, her curly hair bouncing with each shake. "You understand me, Ho? I'm the wrong fucking one!" As Vayda's face began to turn blue, she tried to claw at his face. Pavielle thwarted her assault by shaking his head. He'd gone off the deep end. The nigga left this realm and had dove head first into the mouth of madness. Vayda fought for her life, but after a while she'd began to feel weak. She felt light headed and believed she was about to faint, but actually she was about to die.

The wail of his newborn son snatched Pavielle back in this place and time. He blinked his eyes and looked around. It was as if he was trying to get a grip on things and see exactly where he was. When he realized his hands were wrapped around Vayda's neck, he snatched them away from her. He looked at his hands as if they weren't apart of his body, while Vayda was at his feet on her hands and knees, gasping for air.

"Nasheed," Pavielle started out of the bedroom to attend to his son, but stopped at the doorway when Vayda spoke.

"No, stay away from him, you just keep away!" Vayda grabbed a hold of the nightstand and pulled herself upon her feet. She staggered towards the doorway. Pavielle tried to help her but she snatched her arm away. "Don't touch me, don't chu ever fucking touch me, again!"

She continued out of the bedroom to attend to their child. Realizing that he had fucked up putting his hands on his lady, he pounded the back of his head against the wall and slid down to the floor. He clutched the sides of his head and cursed himself for what he had done.

$$$

The warmth and bright rays of the sun shining upon his eyelids caused them to flutter like a butterfly's wings. He felt the spot that his significant other usually laid, but it was void of her form and heat. His head whipped to the right and she was gone. Pavielle sat up in bed, calling out his lover's name. When she didn't answer, he checked Nasheed's bedroom and then the rest of the house. Vayda was gone. Pavielle headed back into his bedroom and picked up his cell phone. He scrolled through his long list of contacts until he located the name he was looking for. He then tapped the name and placed the cell phone to his ear.

We're sorry but the number you have reached is disconnected or is no longer in service...Said the automated voice recording service.

Pavielle shrugged his shoulders, ended the call and sat the cell phone down on the dresser. He then picked up his Cognac stained glass and a glass bottle containing the dark liquor. He poured himself a drink and took a casual sip. He wasn't worried about the sudden disappearance of his fiancé in the least bit. He didn't have an idea of where she'd gone but he knew that he was going to use every means at his disposal to find her and his baby boy. If Vayda thought she was going to slip in and out of his life that easily, she had another thing coming.

One week later

Pavielle relaxed inside of the theater room of his mansion. The theater was dark save for the light shining in on his face from the projector screen. He was shit faced as usual, but he was able to focus on the *Paid in Full* movie, which was playing out before his glassy, red eyes. Occasionally his eyes would shift down from the screen to the L he was rolling. He'd just licked the brown wrapping closed and was sweeping the flame of a lighter back and forth underneath it, when he heard the screams of a woman and a struggle heading towards his way. He didn't bother to look over his shoulder, because he already knew who it was. Pavielle slipped the L between his lips and put fire to the end of it. He'd just taken a pull and blew out a cloud of white smoke, when Cicero and Maddy came dragging Vayda before him.

"Let me go!" Vayda snatched her arm away from Cicero and slapped him across the face, the impact whipped his head around. Cicero frowned and clenched his jaws, fighting the urge to put his hands on Vayda after her assault.

"No this broad didn't just..." Maddy went to grab Vayda, but Cicero placed a hand to her chest.

"Don't wet it; it's all a part of the job, Sis." Cicero told his older sibling. "Come on, let's bounce. I need a drink."

Maddy and Vayda stared daggers at one another as Cicero pulled her along by her arm. They didn't break contact until Cicero and she had slipped out of the theater's entrance.

Once Cicero and Maddy left, Vayda's eyes fell back on Pavielle. She mad dogged him and folded her arms across her chest, shifting her weight from her left to her right leg. Pavielle ignored her and continued to smoke his blunt, acting as if she wasn't even present. It wasn't until she stepped in his line of vision and blocked his view of the screen that he looked up into her eyes. And when he did he blew a roar of white smoke into her face, disrespectfully.

"You know you wasted your time having them bring me back here, 'cause all I'ma do is leave again. I don't want you and I don't love you anymore." She said that shit trying to crush a nigga'z soul.

"That's fine." Pavielle replied. "Before you came along I got along just fine without your love and I'll be OK without it again." Vayda shot him a deadly look. "What? You thought I was gone be on some old 'baby, please don't leave me, I wouldn't be able to do without you type of shit?' Fuck outta here." He waved her off. "If you wanna leave, then go right ahead, but you leave my son right where he is. If you run off with him again, I assure you I'll track you down and leave you where ever I find you with two bullets in the back of your skull." He stared her dead in her eyes, meaning every word that came from between his lips.

Pavielle glanced over his shoulder once he'd heard his baby boy crying out in the hall. He turned back around to Vayda and said, "Bring me my son." As Vayda traveled up the aisle heading out of the theater, Pavielle took one more pull of his blunt before mashing it out into the ashtray. He sat the ashtray down at his feet and took his son into his arms as he was passed to him. He took his bottle from Vayda and placed it into the baby's mouth, silencing his cries. Pavielle looked down at his son as he sucked on the nipple of the bottle. His eyes were closed and he looked so peaceful. A smirk surfaced upon Pavielle's face and he kissed his baby boy on his chubby cheek. He then looked up at Vayda like *'Bitch, what the fuck are you still doing here?'* before saying, "Oh, you can gone about your business now. I'd like to spend some quality time with my son."

Vayda stormed up the aisle, pissed off. Pavielle lie back in the brown leather theater chair feeding his son and watching *Paid in Full.*

TEN

The next day

Chingo walked around the Del Amo mall with his baby momma, Yvette. Her hands were filled with shopping mall bags being as she'd been to nearly every store inside of the establishment. She was hyped up and ready to keep going, but Chingo and their two year old son, Blessyn, were past ready to go.

"Yvette, I'm ready to get up outta here." Chingo said. "My feet are killing me and lil' man done fell asleep." He nudged his son, who was lying on his shoulder asleep. Drool had run from the corner of his mouth and stained Chingo's blue sweatshirt.

"OK, Boo, let me just run into this last store and then we can leave. I wanna see if they got in this dress I've been looking for." Yvette said from behind her oversized designer shades. She had a shapely figure and breasts the size of coconuts. Her face looked like it belonged on a female R&B artist's album cover.

"You said that three stores ago, Man. Look, do your thang, me and junior will be out in the car." He switched the shopping mall bag from his right to his left wrist before dipping into the pocket of his True Religion's and withdrawing a thick knot of Benjamin Franklins. He peeled off ten of them and passed them to her.

"Alright," She replied, before kissing her slumbering son on the side of his head and then her man on the lips. The couple then parted and went their separate ways.

$$$

Chingo placed his son into the baby seat and secured the safety belt around him. He pecked the little dude on his forehead and ruffled his curly hair before closing the backseat door. He made his way around the back of the car and hopped behind the wheel. The day was pretty hot so he decided to keep the windows up and turn on the air conditioning. He turned the stereo on and surfed through the channels until he found a Hip-Hop station. He turned to his left to grab the handle to let the seat back when a flicker of movement caught his attention. He looked up and a menacing looking man had just run upon his door. The man's gloved hands clutched twin Berettas that were cocked, locked and ready; the sun's rays bounced off of the weapons and casted a colorful rainbow. Chingo's eyes bulged, his heart dropped and he felt his stomach quake. His banger was on his waistline, but to try his hand at a game of chance now would be idiotic. He was sure the cat clutching the Berettas would have clapped him up something awful if he'd attempted to make the slightest of movement. Homeboy had him dead to rights. He couldn't help but think of all of the cats he'd caught with their pants down. You live by the gun then you die by the gun. It was time he had a dose of his own medicine.

Chingo closed his eyes and waited for the hot-ones to mangle his form. A few moments had passed and nothing happened. He opened one eye and looked around, and then he opened the other. The Beretta clutching man had vanished. Chingo heard a car burning rubber out of the parking lot. He reached over into the backseat, removed the safety belt from around his son and the straps that kept him inside the baby seat. He cradled him in his arms, holding him tight. He closed his eyes and thanked God he'd lived to hold his baby boy again.

$$$

"Where is this nigga, Man? Shit," a young man wiped the sweat from his forehead with the back of his hand. "It's hotta than five fat bitches in a Ford Escort out here."

"Be patient, we got this in the bag. All we've gotta do is wait 'til he comes out." A tall man said. His eyes were focused on the mall's exit. His gloved hands were wrapped around the handles of dual Berettas.

The tall man had gotten a call from one of the homegirls claiming she'd saw a reputable from the other side in traffic. The tall man ordered her to tail the target and text his location once he'd arrived at his destination. The homegirl found herself at the Del Amo mall out in Torrance. She didn't waste any time shooting a text to the tall man. She wanted in on the action, but he assured her he and his comrade had it from there.

Seeing something through the windshield, the young man leaned over the steering-wheel and peered closely. "Yo, that's him right there?"

"Where?" The tall man scanned the area.

"Right there?" he pointed to their target who was coming around his car to get into the driver seat.

"How did I miss him coming out?"

"Fool must have come out with that crowd."

The tall man surveyed his surroundings making sure there weren't any witnesses in sight. "I'm finna get'em up outta here." The tall man opened the door and was about to hop out, when the young man grabbed his arm. The tall man looked to his partner and asked, "What's up?"

"Ain't chu gone mask up?"

"Nah, I want this nigga to see who did 'em."

The tall man pulled his arm back and hopped out of the car. He stooped low as he ran towards the whip his target was inside. His target was surfing through the channels of the stereo and had just turned around. His mouth dropped open and his eyes nearly popped out of his head like a pair of those funny glasses, when he saw the tall man gripping the twin Berettas. The target closed his eyes and waited for the shots that were to snatch him from this life. The tall man's face contorted into a vengeful scowl. His fingers had just brushed against the triggers, when something in the corner of his eye caught his attention. He looked to the backseat and there was a sleeping toddler. The scowl he wore gave to a surprised expression. The kid couldn't be any older than two or three years old. The tall man's eyes darted from the kid to his target before he finally took off running back in the direction he came.

"Go! Go!" Gouch slapped the dashboard after hopping back into the G-ride. Killa Dre quickly resurrected the engine and burned rubber out of the parking lot. He swung out into traffic recklessly, but slowed to a moderate speed before crossing the light ahead.

"What happened?" Killa Dre asked.

"He had a kid with 'em," Gouch answered.

ELEVEN

Paybacc sat on the beat up flower printed sofa, fogging the gold urn with his breath and polishing it to a shine. Satisfied that he could see his reflection in the urn, he sat it on the coffee table.

"I'll be right back, Loco, let me check in on the young cousins over here." He patted the urn and entered the kitchen. He stepped behind his young boys, placing a large hand on the back of both of their chairs. He looked over their shoulders as they sat at the kitchen table, chopping rocks from an off white crack cookie and packing them into plastic sandwich bags. Shadow and Steel were two of the young cats Paybacc had taken a liking to since his release from prison. He decided to take them under his wing like he'd done with Nightmare, Domino, Reboc and many others.

"Y'all almost done?" Paybacc asked, picking up the smoldering L from the ashtray at the center of the table. He took a pull from the blunt and expelled white smoke into his nostrils and back out again.

"Yeah," Shadow wiped his sweaty forehead with the back of the hand he held the razor blade in. "After this lil'bit, we're done."

"Yo, let me hit that." Steel took the blunt from Paybacc and took a few puffs.

"Y'all call that nigga Bad Lucc?" Paybacc asked, looking between his little homies.

"Yep, dude on his way now. It took 'em a minute but he got rid of that first shit we hit'em with. It's hotter than teenage pussy out there."

Knock! Knock! Knock! Knock!

The rapping at the door snatched every ones attention. Steel grabbed his thang and pushed away from the table, about to see who their visitor was.

"Chill, Steel, I got it." Paybacc said, "Y'all niggaz finish that up."

Paybacc snatched his joint off of the coffee table where he'd left it beside the gold urn and approached the front door. "Who is it?" he called out.

"It's Chingo, Cuz." A voice responded.

Paybacc unlocked the door and snatched it open. Once Chingo was inside he closed and locked it back. The two men slapped hands and embraced one another.

"What's cracking, Gangsta?"

"I almost got blasted at the Del Amo today." Chingo told him. With that said, Shadow and Steel came over.

Paybacc frowned and folded his arms across to his chest. "What happened?"

"I had just came outta the mall and hopped into my shit. I turned on the stereo and when I turn around this mothafucka Gouch is right up on my window. With two thangs," he outstretched both arms and made his hands into the shapes of guns, "I thought that was it for me, Cuz. I just knew I was on my way. I close my eyes and waited to hear them thangs exploding in my ears, but it never happens. I look around and the nigga had upped and vanished."

"From the shit I done heard about that fool, I'm amazed to see you standing here right now." Shadow said. "That dude is official like a referee with a whistle."

"Straight up, that's one Dead Rag that don't play." Steel nodded in agreement.

"Man, I think he only let me keep my life 'cause I had my son in the baby seat in the car." Chingo informed them.

"You had your seed with chu?" Paybacc inquired.

"Yeah, him and my Baby Momma," Chingo explained, as he dipped his hand into his pocket and pulled out a vial of coke. "She was taking forever and a day, so I left her in the mall and bounced with junior to the car."

"A killer with a conscience doesn't have any place in this war," Paybacc looked to the gold urn. "Ain't that right, Domino?" Steel and Shadow exchanged glances like *This mothafucka done lost his mind,*' but Chingo didn't bat an eye. He was used to this sort of behavior from Paybacc. He hadn't been right in the head since Domino had been killed. Paybacc had always been a dangerous man, but with Domino's death he had become double the threat.

"I'll tell you one thing, where he showed mercy I won't." Paybacc assured him. "If I was to ever catch Booby or his broad I'd quickly do away with them. I took the kiddy gloves off once I lost my sons." He spoke of the deaths of Nightmare and Domino. Paybacc saying this caused Shadow's forehead to wrinkle. He thought Paybacc was off the chain when he heard he'd chopped some teenager's feet off and had a couple of the homies toss them over a power-line. If that was child's play to him then he wondered what other wicked thoughts were formulating inside of that head of his.

"The longer this war stretches, the greater of the chances of one of us getting taken off of our feet." Chingo tapped a little coke out onto his fist and snorted it like a pro. He then sniffed and thumbed his nose; his eyes became glassy and moist. "The clouds parted and the sun shined on my ass this time, but who's to say that it will happen again? Know what I'm saying?"

"I know exactly what you're saying." Payback took the vial from Chingo and tapped some of the coke out onto his fist and snorted it too. He then bent his neck from left to right, causing the bones to crack in it. "You don't have anything to worry about, Loco. I've already got someone on your boy Booby. That Dead Rag is living on borrowed time and doesn't even know it." He smirked. "Everything is going to be just beautiful, you just wait and see."

Paybacc looked at his reflection in the urn. He clenched his teeth and checked them for any food particles. He turned back around and Shadow and Steel where lounging about on the living room couch. "Fuck are you two niggaz doing? Get back to that work. Chop! Chop!" he clapped his hands and the young wolves went back to their occupation.

"I'm outta here, Cuz." Chingo rose to his feet, stuffing the vial of coke into his pocket. He slapped hands with the homies before making a beeline for the door.

"Chingo," Paybacc called after him and he turned around. "Watch yourself out there, Cousin."

Chingo nodded and stepped out of the door.

$$$

Yvette sat in the front passenger seat of the family van that Chingo had rented. Her eyes were rimmed red and had swollen so much from crying that she looked like an insect. Her hand trembled as she brought a cigarette to her pink lipstick lips and took a pull, drawing the toxi smoke into her lungs. She allowed the white smoke to circulate around in her lungs before blowing it back out. Yvette looked to the Glock .50 in the palm of her manicured hand and then to the backseat at the life it was meant to protect. Blessyn, her baby boy, was fast asleep. For a time she sat there watching his tiny chest rise and fall as he took breaths. He was so beautiful and precious to her. A slight smirk formed on Yvette's face watching him sleep so peacefully. She knew that if it came down to it that she'd kill and die, all for him.

Yvette leaned over into the backseat and placed a gentle kiss on her baby boy's forehead. As she was pulling back she heard a knock on the driver side window that startled her. Swiftly, she fell back into the front passenger seat and pointed the Glock at the window, ready to twist a Fuck-Nigga's cap.

Chingo jumped back from the window with his hands up in surrender when Yvetter pointed the gun at him. Realizing who it was Yvette sighed with relief. She lowered her weapon and pressed the button that triggered the lock mechanism. The locks shot up and Chingo snatched open the door. Removing his banger from his waistline, he slid into the driver's seat and slammed the door shut. Yvette lunged at him, wrapping her arms around him and squeezing tight. This caught him off guard, but he caressed her back and allowed her to sob. He could tell that she was scared, which was why he didn't have any second thoughts about what he was about to do. Once Yvette had gotten it all out, she sat back into the passenger seat and wiped her wet face with the back of her hand.

"You, all right?" Chingo asked, giving her thigh a slight squeeze.

She nodded.

"Everything is going to be all right, you just watch." Chingo told her. "I just need for you and lil' man to lay low out here at cha aunt's house for a while until I settle shit up out here. I'ma Hot Boy in the hood right now, Yvette. Niggaz are gunning for me and I can't have y'all out here. I know you don't want to go but it's for the good of this family, alright?"

Yvette nodded and looked to the backseat at the luggage she'd packed for herself and the baby. She even packed a few more things for Chingo in case he changed his mind and decided to make the trip with them.

"OK," She looked to Chingo, "Alright."

Chingo tilted her chin up with his finger and kissed her tenderly. He then resurrected the van and pulled off.

TWELVE

"You didn't take 'em out?" Pavielle asked, holding the driver's door of his Benz open as he was about to hop in. Gouch and Killa Dre stood before him. This was an hour after they pulled out of the mission operation 'Kill Chingo'.

Gouch looked to Killa Dre then back to Pavielle. He shook his head and replied, "No."

Pavielle frowned and asked, "Why?"

"He had his lil' boy in the backseat."

Pavielle's face twisted and he bit down on his bottom lip. The veins in his forehead and neck bulged as he balled his fist tight; slamming it down upon the roof of his Mercedes. The sudden action startled Gouch and Killa Dre. "Fuck him and his son! You should have laid 'em both!" he motioned a finger between Gouch and Killa Dre. "Lil' nigga could grow up to be a crab like his daddy and end up murking my son, or one of the homies." Gouch looked at Pavielle like he couldn't believe he just said that. "Don't look at me like that 'cause you know damn well that it'll most likely happen. We were born into this shit and we picked up flags, so it's not farfetched. You should have killed that boy, Gucci. Chingo is about money and murder. You probably let go of the nigga that's to be my downfall."

"There's always next time." Gouch said.

"There might not be a next time." Pavielle shot back. He blew hard and brought his hand down his face. He was frustrated and stressed the fuck out.

Pavielle's cell phone rang and vibrated. He answered it.

"Talk to me," he listened to what he was being told. "I'm on my way now." He disconnected the call and looked to Gouch. "Look, I got some shit I gotta handle. We'll chop it up later."

"You want us to roll?" Gouch asked.

"Nah, I need some time alone so I can think."

"Alright."

Pavielle dapped up Gouch and Killa Dre before ducking off into his car and driving off.

Pavielle stood beside his Benz leaning all of his weight upon a cane. He patiently awaited the arrival of his acquaintance while he smoked an L. He'd occasionally glance at his presidential Rolex. Fifteen minutes had passed and the cat he was supposed to meet inside of the old warehouse hadn't arrived. After flicking what was left of the blunt aside and expelling white smoke from his nose and mouth, he dipped his hand into his pocket. As soon as he brandished his cell phone he was blinded by the headlights of a Lincoln Town Car as it entered the old warehouse. He could hear the crunching of gravel under the vehicle's tires as it rolled in his direction. Once the driver had executed the vehicle's headlights, all that could be seen was a mysterious black figure behind the wheel. For a time the figure just sat there and then the driver side door opened. A black leather dress shoe stepped out first, followed by another. A man in glasses and a suede copper brown jacket emerged, with a firm hold on a briefcase. He slammed the door closed and pushed his specs back upon his nose before starting in Pavielle's direction.

The man stopped before Pavielle and he took a good look at him. He was about fifty to sixty years old with skin the color of mahogany. His head was shaven and covered in white stubble. Pavielle could tell from his physique that he was in good shape and most likely watched what he ate.

"Please excuse my tardiness; I caught a flat on my way over." The man spoke with a husky voice.

"Don't worry about it; do you have that for me?" Pavielle asked.

"Yes, it's right here." The man sat the briefcase on the hood of Pavielle's Benz and popped its locks. He opened the lid of the briefcase and turned it around to the man that had hired him for his services. Pavielle went through the I.Ds, social security cards, and passports that lie inside. Satisfied with the merchandise, he tossed them back into the briefcase and closed it. He then picked the briefcase up from the hood of the car and tossed the man a bankroll of dead presidents secured by a rubber-band. The man looked at the bankroll before depositing it into a pocket inside of his suede jacket.

"Take it easy." Pavielle turned and opened the driver side door of his car.

"Mr. Smith." The man called after him. Pavielle turned around and threw his head back slightly. "Your situation…Are you sure you want to handle it in this manner? This could get bad for you."

Pavielle frowned. "How so?"

"If those three were to ever get caught, who's to say that one of them, if not all of them, won't sell you up the river?"

"Sell me up the river with what? I don't have anything to do with this. I'm just a dude helping out a few of his friends. The most I could get charged with is aiding and abiding fugitives, but I'm not even gonna chance getting that close. I'll have someone else deliver these goodies." He slightly lifted the briefcase.

"Mr. Smith, I make it my business to know everything there is to know about my clients and their affairs. I know who you are and I'm aware of the type of business you're involved in." The man informed Pavielle.

Pavielle slammed the door closed and approached the man. "Exactly what is it that you think you know about me, Old Man?"

"For instance, your real name is Pavielle Hood. You're a drug kingpin and the leader of a Blood gang called the Outlaws. You have a fiancé named Vayda, a newborn son named Nasheed and an older brother named Gouch. A couple of weeks ago your uncle was killed. And he's the reason why your part of town has been plagued with a rash of murders. You've ordered these hits. You want revenge, and the bodies won't stop dropping until you're satisfied." The man folded his arms to his chest and said, "Should I keep going?" He got his answer through Pavielle's silence. "OK then. Like I was saying, you can help these friends of yours escape to whatever place you have in mind, but there is a chance that they can be discovered. If they're captured and taken into custody there is a great possibility that they'll use you as a bargaining chip. They could tell the authorities that you ordered them to lay down those hits, or say that you're supplying them with drugs. Whatever information that they may have that could lighten their sentences, do you follow me?"

Pavielle waved him off and said, "I'm not worry about that, my soldiers are solid. They'll never break or fold. I stand by mine a hundred percent."

The man chuckled and shook his head. "Then you're a fool. Don't ever put that much faith into anyone. They'll let chu down every time. Most people can only be loyal to themselves. Stand up guys are few and far in between. Our numbers are dwindling and we're slowly dying out and becoming extinct." He rose from the hood of his car. "I can take care of the lot of them; make it quick and painless. All you'll have to do is give me the green-light and it's a done deal." He studied Pavielle's face and could tell that he was thinking on it. "Their fates rests in your hands, it's your call."

Coming to his conclusion, Pavielle shook his head. "Nah, I'ma ride it out with my goons."

"Suit yourself." The man said. "You got my number if you change your mind."

He hopped back behind the wheel, resurrected the engine, swung around and rolled out of the warehouse. Pavielle stood outside of his car pondering; the man's words had left him with much to think about. He hoped his final decision would be the right one.

$$$

Vadya lay in bed beside Pavielle listening to his breathing as he slept. Her eyes were fixated on the tattoo on the inside of her wrist **RIDE OR DIE**. She and Pavielle had gotten the ink on the same day, in the same place. It symbolized their love and devotion to one another. It meant that they would have each other's back no matter the circumstances. When things got drastic, they could find solace within one another. They trusted and believed in one another whole heartedly, either one would die preserve the life of the other without a second thought. They had a bond and a kindred ship that seemed to be unbreakable, but now Vayda was starting feel otherwise. She wanted to get as far away from Pavielle as possible. And though he had given her his blessings to go along with her life as she pleased, there was no way she was leaving her baby behind. Vayda was feeling suffocated being with Pavielle. It was like she was in the middle of an ocean with a 1,000 lb boulder shackled to her ankle. It didn't matter how hard she tried to get away, it was there weighing her down and minimizing her movements. Vayda knew that the only way she'd ever be able to take her baby without having to live a life on the run from Pavielle's goons was to murder him. It was her Ace in the hole, the card up her sleeve. Her back was against the wall and she was desperate. This was her last chance and she was going to play her trump card.

Vayda eased out of the bed and snuck into the walk-in closet. She retrieved the .22 with the ivory handle from the bottom dresser drawer. Once she made sure that its magazine was fully loaded, she gently pushed it back into the bottom of the weapon, and slowly chambered a round into it. She then emerged from the walk-in closet, walking briskfully in Pavielle's direction. She crawled into the bed and stood upon her knees. She then closed her eyes tight, turned her head and pointed the sleek, black pistol at Pavielle's head. Her hand slightly trembled as she began to apply pressure to the trigger. Tears came bursting from her eyes and escaping down her rose gold cheeks. She bit down on her bottom lip, trying to find the balls to steal the life of the man she'd loved unconditionally. Vayda's head whipped back around to Pavielle and she saw her hand holding the .22 to his dome. She wiped her wet face with the back of her hand and gripped the weapon with both hands. She took a couple of deep breaths, telling herself that she was going to pull the trigger at the count of three. One…Two…Three, she counted in her head and made to hug the trigger with all she could muster. Suddenly, she lowered the .22 and sobbed as quietly as she could. Once whimpers escaped her lips that were loud enough to wake Pavielle, she jumped out of bed and rushed to the bathroom. Inside she turned on the shower head and dashed over into the corner. Still, gripping the .22 in her hand she hugged her legs to her chest and bawled like a baby. Her face reddened and her eyes pinked as tears cascaded down her cheeks.

"I…I still love him…" she croaked. "Oh God, I still do. But I don't want to no more." She banged her head up against the wall, hating to still be so much in love with a man that had wronged her.

Pavielle squirmed around in the bed until eventually his eyes opened. He turned over and saw that Vayda wasn't by his side. Hearing the shower head running inside of the bathroom, he thought nothing of it and rolled back over. He closed his eyes and waited for sleep to invade him. He hadn't the slightest clue that he was a stone's throw away from the afterlife. Even if you would have told him he wouldn't have believed it.

THIRTEEN

G-thang, Voodoo, and Dip had gotten settled at Pavielle's spot in Ladera Heights. The cable, water, and power were still on, but the only thing in the refrigerator was a box of Arm & Hammer bacon soda. Voodoo peeled Vida off a few bills and sent her to the super market. Vida returned with mostly junk food and TV dinners seeing as how no one in the house could cook. Later on that night the gang camped out in the living room eating DiGiorno's pizza and watching Love and Hip-hop New York.

While everyone was kicking it out in the living room, Dip was inside of the bathroom submerged in a tub of hot, sudsy water. Being alone had given Dip plenty of time to think to himself. Though he thought about having to be on the run for the rest of his life, oddly that was the least of his worries. He was more concerned about the little girl he'd robbed of a future. It was because of him that she'd never experience her first kiss, go to prom, or drive her first car. All of that was snatched right from under her like a cheap rug. And it was his fault.

Every time Dip dozed off inside of the tub his mental was assaulted with images of the little girl he'd murdered. The images were painful and stung his brain like a million tips of hot needles. Every minute of every hour he thought about the poor girl and what he had done to her. His conscience wouldn't give him a break. He thought he could combat his guilt with alcohol and drugs but they only made it worse. Dip thought the only way for him to escape his misery was for him to sever his ties from this life so that he could hopefully find peace in the next. And so he found himself relaxing in the tub with a razor he'd plucked fresh from the box.

Dip lay back in the tub holding a razor in one hand and staring at the wrist of his other. He opened and closed his palm, trying to find a sufficient vein to sever. "Come on, come on." Dip frowned and clenched his jaws, as he closed and opened his palm. He balled his fist this last time and a nice, juicy vein formed before his eyes. "There you go." He whispered, holding his fist closed as tight as he could. He lifted the razor and the light from the ceiling bounced off it, causing it to twinkle. In one swift motion, he swiped the razor across his vein and sent blood squirting wildly. Dip bit down on his bottom lip trying to fight the pain as his blood hit the water and began turning it orange.

Knocks at the door startled Dip. He snatched the red bandana from the back pocket of his Dickies, which were lying on the floor, and tied it around his wrist to stop the blood flow. He then tried his best to gather his wits, before he addressed whoever was at the door.

"Who is it?" Dip hollered out.

"It's Voodoo, Blood, I gotta take a piss."

Dip hid his bandana tied wrist in the sudsy water.

"All right, come in."

Voodoo ran inside of the bathroom clutching a Source magazine and a green pill bottle loaded with Kush. Hurriedly, she unbuckled her belt and pulled down her jeans and boxers. She plopped down on the commode and went about the task of rolling a blunt. Once she was done, she fired it up and shared it with Dip. They politicked while indulging in some of Cali's finest. Voodoo hadn't a clue that her closest comrade had attempted suicide just minutes ago.

$$$

Ziggy stood at the medicine cabinet mirror staring at his reflection. Every since Pavielle and his goons rolled out in his rides he'd been catching heat from his wife. She had suspicions of his gambling again. She didn't want to believe it but her instincts were screaming it at her. They were already in a financial strain so she figured that he'd sold off the cars to pay his debts. It took some reasoning but Ziggy was able to convince her that he'd taken the cars to get some work done on them and that they'd be back in another week or two. At first Shantira didn't believe him, but then he swore on his mother's grave. If you knew Ziggy you'd know that he never swore on his mother's grave unless he was telling you the truth. It was the only way you could tell if he was bullshitting you or not.

Now that Ziggy had the misses out of his hair he had the business with Pavielle he had to attend to. He'd taken out a loan on a couple of his properties and all he was waiting on now was the check to be cut. Once he'd gotten the currency he was going to deliver it to Pavielle and have him sign his vehicles back over to him. Once all of this was taken care of Ziggy could go back to running his company and living his extraordinary life. Boy, he couldn't wait.

After soaping up his hands, Ziggy turned on the bathroom faucet and rinsed his mitts under the flowing water. He'd just turned off the faucet and had begun drying his hands, when he heard a knock at the door.

"What is it?" Ziggy hollered out.

"Dinner's ready." Shantira told him.

"Be out in a minute." Ziggy replied. He gave himself one more look in the mirror before pulling open the door and taking his leave.

FOURTEEN

"Look at these niggaz, Boy, kicking it on the porch like they don't know what time it is out here." Wimp shook his head and guzzled some of the Mad Dog 20/20 from the tall can. He belched and sat the can on the floor between his sneakers. He was a tall, yellow skinned cat with beaded brown hair and a bunch of tattoo on his face that didn't mean much of anything. Upon first glance you would have thought he'd gotten drunk and given a couple of kids tattoo guns and allowed them to do whatever they pleased with his face.

"My dude, your breath smells like hot vomit and musty armpits." Crazy Eyez winced from the foul stench of his homeboy's breath. He was sitting in the front passenger seat studying the movements of their intended targets. He was a youthful looking cat with thick eyebrows and whiskers that made him resemble a cat. He was wearing a black beanie with Low Bottoms stitched across it and a black sweatshirt.

"Fuck you." Wimp grabbed his .45 automatic from underneath his seat and chambered a round into its head. He looked to Crazy Eyez and he was checking the magazine of his weapon. Once Crazy Eyez saw that the magazine was loaded with shells, he smacked it back into the bottom of the handle and chambered a round into it.

"Ready, Cuz?" Wimp asked.

"Ready is my middle name." Crazy Eyez replied.

The twosome hopped out of the Chevy Trail Blazer and slammed the doors shut. Together, they stooped low and ran towards a house at the end of the block. Upon its porch they spotted two Bloods from around the way known as

Kenny B and Bool Aide. The Red Rags kicked it upon the porch talking about your normal everyday bullshit while sharing a smoldering blunt. The pair was so engrossed in their conversation that they hadn't even notice the two black shapes engaging them. By the time they'd acknowledged the looming danger, Wimp and Crazy Eyez were halfway inside of the yard with their bangers pointed in their direction. Wimp and Crazy Eyez had just approached the stoop and were about to squeeze the triggers of their weapons, when two Bloods emerged from the bushes cradling AK-47s. Wimp and Crazy Eyez were shocked. Their eyes bulged and their mouths dropped open.

"Soooowoooo Gang!" One of the Bloods bellowed.

"Or don't bang!" the other finished.

They hugged the triggers of their AK-47s and ripped holes through Wimp and Crazy Eyez, blood splattering everywhere. Wimp and Crazy Eyez lie on the ground riddled with bullets. Though Wimp was dead, Crazy Eyez was still clinging to life. He coughed up blood as he stared up at the Bloods. They wore red bandanas over the lower halves of their faces. Their terrifying eyes bored down at the lone survivor.

"Surprise, Bitch!" one of the Bloods said. "Didn't think we saw y'all asses circling the block, did you?"

"Like the song said," the other Blood began, pointing his AK-47 at Crazy Eyez' face. "You should have been a B-Dawg."

"This is for the big homie Gangsta, Mothafucka!"

Rat! Tat! Tat! Tat! Tat! Tat! Tat! Tat! Tat!

The firing stopped and the smoke cleared. Crazy Eyez lay sprawled on the ground, bloody and filled with what looked like a million holes. If Crazy Eyez' people were to see him like this they wouldn't even recognize him.

"Help me scoop this nigga up so we can dump 'em in his bitch ass hood." One of the Bloods lugging the AK-47 said to his homie beside him.

$$$

Ricky V. pulled up to his date's house in a white on white, black rag top BMW 760. He popped a Listerine strip into his mouth and let the sun visor flap down so he could use its mirror. He smoothed out his trimmed mustache with his fingers and took the time to admire his 360 waves, before brushing his close fade. When he was done he gave himself the once over and smooched at the sun visor mirror. A smile stretched across his face. He felt that he was the finest mothafucka to have ever worn a pair of Mauri shoes.

Ricky V. pulled a slip of paper from inside of his red blazer and looked over the address. His eyes went from the address on the slip of paper to the address on the house he was parked out in front of. Confirming the address, he folded the slip of paper up and slipped it back inside of his blazer. He then glanced at his Michael Kors watch and honked the horn. From behind the wheel, Ricky V. looked out of the front passenger window at the house. He saw a cute young lady pull back the curtains of the window and look at him, talking on the telephone.

Ricky V. held up the wrist he wore the Michael Kors watch on, pointed at it, and waved the young lady on. He watched as she hung up the telephone and waved goodbye to him. A look of confusion crossed his face. Seeing something at the corner of his eye, he turned to the driver side window just in time to see the glass implode. Bullets shredded his face, neck and shoulder, killing him instantly. His face crashed into the horn and caused it to blare loudly.

Scurrrrrrr!

A royal blue Denali truck sped through a stop-sign and bent the corner at the end of the block making a successful getaway.

The next day

J-Bone crossed the threshold into the liquor store, casting evil eyes at the Korean owner posted behind the bulletproof glass. He hated the 66 year old man with every cell of his being. He didn't make it a secret that he despised the black faces that frequented his store, even though they gave him majority of his business. Not only was the owner a racist, but he sold his merchandise at ridiculous prices. Seeing as how the next liquor store was eight blocks away and no one wanted to trek that far for a pack of smokes and whatever else they desired, Tom's Deli & Mini Mart was convenient.

J-Bone grabbed a Brisk Raspberry tea out of the refrigerator and a bag of Funions, before making his way to the counter. As the Korean clerk rang up his items, his eyes scanned over the selection of liquor and tobacco behind the counter.

"Let me get a 5th of that Hen-Dog and uh…" he massaged his chin as he tried to make his decision. "A box of…"

Boom!

The front of J-Bone's face splattered against the bulletproof glass. His body stumbled forth, crashing into a rack of potato chips and hitting the floor. The gunman stood behind him gripping a silver .44 Magnum revolver. He wore a Michael Myers mask and a red Champion hoodie. The gunman stepped to J-Bone's limp form and gave him two more to the back of the dome just cause. He looked up at the Korean clerk and saw that he was visibly shaken. He was about to send some heat his way until he realized that he was shielded by the bulletproof glass. The gunman tucked his warm banger on his waistline and casually strode outside. He hopped on his Huffy mountain bike and rode off.

Killa Dre pulled off the Michael Myers mask as he rode inside of the alley. He hid the Huffy bike in a pile of black garbage bags and peeled off his clothes. He tossed his clothes into a trash bin along with a mask. The entire time he was completing this task he was wearing his boxer-briefs and talking on his cell phone.

"…Yeah, I'll be out here." Killa Dre disconnected the call. He then soaked his clothes and the Michael Myers mask with charcoal fuel. He tossed the charcoal fuel aside, pulled out a book of matches and struck a match. A flame was brought forth. He was just about to toss the burning match inside of the trash bin when…

Vroom!

Vroom!

Vroom!

Vroom!

Four police cruisers ripped past the alley and sent debris into the air. Killa Dre froze holding the burning match pinched between his finger and thumb. He knew that they were more than likely en route to the body he'd left at Tom's

Deli & Mini Mart. Once he was sure that the coast was clear, he tossed the burning match into the trash bin.

Froooosh!

Killa Dre pulled a black garbage bag out from where it was hidden beneath a bunch of others. He removed the clothes it concealed and got dressed as fast as he could. Once he was fully clothed, he tucked a fresh .44 Magnum revolver into the small of his back. He then walked towards the mouth of the alley, sucking on a cherry Tootsi Roll pop.

A '64 white Chevy Impala with blood red interior pulled across the mouth of the alley. Killa Dre snatched open the door and plopped down into the front passenger seat. As soon as he slammed the door shut the old school vehicle drove off.

"So, where are we headed?" Killa Dre asked.

"Today's pickup," Gouch told him. "Or have you forgotten?"

"That's right, my bad."

Gouch looked to Killa Dre and saw the sheen of sweat on his forehead.

"Why you sweating like you've been exercising?"

"I have been exercising…My trigger-finger,Blood." Killa Dre smirked, coiling and uncoiling his trigger-finger.

Gouch cracked a smile and shook his head.

FIFTEEN

Pavielle sat inside of his living room with his feet propped upon the coffee table. He slowly sipped a glass of Cognac as he flipped through the cable channels. Lying beside his feet were a flip cell phone and a second sim chip. His cell phone rang and danced across the table. His eyes darted to the cell phone's screen and saw that it had "Unavailable" on it. The cell phone rang a total of three times before going still and three "Missed Calls" appeared on the screen. Pavielle sat up and placed his glass on the coffee table. He snatched up his cell phone and replaced its sim chip with the one on the coffee table. He then dialed a number that he remembered from memory. The phone rang twice before someone answered.

"It ain't here."

"Fuck you mean it ain't there, Gucci?"

"Like I said, 'it ain't here'," Gouch made himself clear. "What chu want me to do?"

"Something is up." Pavielle figured, massaging his chin. "This has never happened. It's always there."

"Well, it ain't here today," Gouch told him. "Me and Killa have been out here for an hour."

"Let me call you back, I'ma hit this fool Bullet up and see what's good."

"Don't waste your time." Gouch told him. "I hit his jack and B.J's, and neither one of their numbers working. They changed their numbers on us, so you know what this means, right?"

"Yeah, we've been cut off." Pavielle came to the realization. He massaged the bridge of his nose. "Alright, y'all niggaz bring it in, Man. We may have to roll out there and see this nigga."

"Alright," Gouch said before hanging up.

Pavielle sat his cell phone on the coffee table. He then blew hard and brought both of his hands down his face. When he looked up Vayda was placing a plate of food down before him. It consisted of smothered pork chops with mushrooms and onions, steamed broccoli, and macaroni and cheese. Beside the plate she placed a glass of red wine.

"What's this?" Pavielle asked, picking over the plate of food with his fork.

"Dinner," Vayda replied. She'd just returned from the kitchen with a glass of wine and a plate of her own. She sat down beside him. You could tell that she was still hot at him. The tension between them was thick.

"Thanks." He pecked her on the cheek. He went to take a bite of the broccoli when he saw her watching him. He closed his mouth and dropped the fork down in the plate. "You did something to my food, didn't you? I bet chu poisoned it." Vayda gave him the evil eye as she chewed on a piece of pork chop. This made Pavielle reluctant to take a bite of his meal. "I'm cool on this food." He pushed the plate away from him. He picked up the glass of wine and sniffed it. He was about to take a sip until he saw that Vayda was still watching him. "You spit in this?"

Vayda sighed and rolled her eyes.

"Stop fucking up and you wouldn't have to worry about if I did something to your food or not." She focused her attention on the flat-screen and continued the consumption of her meal.

"Whatever, Vayda, I'm not beat for this shit." Pavielle threw back the last of his Cognac. He then grabbed his cane and pulled himself up from the couch. He shuffled off to get dressed so that he could roll out to Black Jesus' crib.

$$$

Gouch drove out to Black Jesus' mansion with Pavielle riding shotgun. Pavielle fired up an L and watched the transformation of the scenery through the passenger window. He played the role of the quiet thinker most of the way while Gouch listened to music. It wasn't until they pulled up to the giant golden gates of Black Jesus' estate that Pavielle looked alive. He passed his blunt to Gouch and motioned the guard over. The husky Mexican man shuffled over and leaned forth, meeting Pavielle at eye level at the window. He was clad in a black cap and matching fatigues. An M-16 was slung over his shoulder and a pistol was resting inside of the holster on his waistline.

"How are you?" Pavielle greeted the guard. "My name is Booby; I'm here to see Jesus Arturo."

The guard nodded and stood erect. He took the walkie talkie from his hip and brought it to his lips. He held down the button and spoke with someone in Spanish. Pavielle could tell by the sound of the other voice that it was Black Jesus. He couldn't understand what he was saying but from the tone of his voice he knew that he wasn't too happy. By this time Gouch was listening in too.

"As a matter of fact, let me speak with him." Pavielle heard Black Jesus' say. The guard passed the walkie talkie to Pavielle and showed him how to use it.

"Booby, are you there?" Black Jesus spoke again.

"Yeah, I'm here," Pavielle replied, "Your people missed that drop, Fam. I've been trying to get a hold of you, but your number is not working."

"There won't be any more business between us." Black Jesus said seriously. "Your lack of respect has led me to several ties with you.

"What?" Pavielle spat like he had a bad taste in his mouth.

Gouch shook his head shamefully. He had tried to tell his baby brother about the disrespect he'd shown Black Jesus but he just wouldn't listen. Now their ties were being severed from a plug that had some of the sweetest cocaine that had ever hit the streets of Cali.

"You heard me, baboso; I'm not fucking with you anymore, until you learn to show me respect." Black Jesus told him. "It's out of love and respect for your uncle that you aren't hanging from the meat hook inside of some freezer with a couple of my men going to work on you with an electrical saw and a power drill."

Pavielle's face twisted with murderous hatred as he listened to Black Jesus. He couldn't wait for the drug lord to finish so he could give him a piece of his mind.

"Fuck you! Fuck you, you piñata beating, border hopping, wetback son of a bitch," Pavielle shouted into the walkie talkie, spittle flying from his lips, "Who the fuck do you think you're talking to? Huh? I'll drive a taco truck through these gates and straight up your fucking ass, Bitch!" Pavielle breathed heavily as he listened for a reply. When he didn't get a response, he waved the guard over. The guard leaned over into the passenger window.

"You didn't hear that?" Pavielle asked through the walkie talkie. "Well, hear this?"

Boc!

A piping hot bullet crashed into the guard's forehead, knocking off his cap and dropping him to the ground. Pavielle hopped out of the Hummer and approached the guard's body. He gripped the walkie talkie in one hand and his banger in the other.

"You hear that? Huh?" Pavielle barked into the walkie talkie. "Huh, mothafucka? What about this!"

Boc! Boc! Boc! Boc! Boc!

Bullets ripped through the dead guard's body and struck the ground beneath him, causing a cloud of dust to manifest and rise into the air.

"Booby, what the fuck, Man?" Gouch shouted from behind the wheel.

"You hear that? Did you hear that, Ese?" Pavielle roared into the walkie talkie and bit down on his bottom lip. He waited to hear Black Jesus response and shortly he got it.

"Yes, I heard it, loud and clear." Black Jesus said. For a moment there was silence and then he spoke again. "You fucked up, Homeboy."

"That's it," Gouch said. "You done it, we're at fucking war now."

Pavielle tossed the walkie talkie aside and hopped into the front passenger seat of the Hummer. Gouch didn't waste any time backing up and speeding off down the road.

$$$

Black Jesus listened to the walkie talkie as he sat behind his desk inside of his study. Bullet sat on top of his desk with his arms folded across his chest, watching him idly.

Boc! Boc! Boc! Boc! Boc!

"Booby, what the fuck, Man?" Gouch's voice came over the walkie talkie, followed by Pavielle's.

"You hear that? Did you hear that, Ese?"

After hearing the gunshots Black Jesus knew that Pavielle had murdered the guard at the front entrance of his estate. He shook his head, hating to hear that Pavielle had blatantly disrespected him once again. He blew hard and held down the button, speaking into the walkie talkie.

"Yes, I heard it, loud and clear." Black Jesus took the time to massage the bridge of his nose before continuing. "You fucked up, Homeboy." He let his arm dropped to his side. All it took was a moment for rage to mount up inside of him. "Fuck!" he threw the walkie talkie as hard as he could at the wall. He smacked a portrait from off of his desk.

"He's gone too far now, Bro, you can't turn a blind eye to this shit." Bullet told his big brother. "Something like this is going to have everyone talking. Your rep is going to come into question."

"You think I don't know that?"

"Clearly, this mothafucka doesn't place any value on his life, so why should you?"

"Shut up!" Black Jesus massaged his temples, feeling a migraine coming on.

"I know what you're thinking, he's Gangsta's nephew, give 'em a pass, but damn, Bro. How many passes are you going to give this kid?"

"I said 'shut the fuck up!'" Black Jesus roared. "I can't hear myself think."

Bullet raised his hands in surrender and plopped down in the chair before the desk.

"Alright then," Black Jesus began, "First thing is first; call someone to have them clean up Javier. The last thing I need is some pinche pig sniffing around here."

"I'm on it." Bullet pulled out his cell and placed a call.

Black Jesus placed his elbows on the desk and put his finger tips and thumbs together. The thought of killing Booby flew back and forth across his mental like a ping pong ball. As things were looking, Gangsta's youngest nephew would probably be coming to join him sooner than either of them thought. Black Jesus sat back in his plush brown leather executive chair thinking, decisions, decisions.

$$$

"Shit just got real," Gouch said from behind the wheel.

"Why do you worry so much?" Pavielle asked as he relit his L.

"Same reason why you drink so fucking much," Gouch fired back.

"I drink 'cause it helps me relax." Pavielle picked the lint from his polyester shirt with the King Tut image on it. He then brushed himself off and took another pull from his blunt.

"Well, you're gonna have to cut the Cognac outta your diet 'cause the troops are gonna need you with a sober mind and thinking." Gouch said seriously. "We aren't dealing with some D-boy from off the block here. This mothafucka is major league. He's as close to a real life Sosa as you're gonna get."

"Blah, blah, blah, blah," Pavielle rolled his eyes. "It's like Biggie said 'Them niggaz bleed just like us.' I'm not stressing over Black Jesus. I got an army and guns, too."

"Yeah, well, that mothafucka has a bigger army and more guns than you, Baby Brother." Gouch informed him. "You need a serious reality check. The homes there could make a phone call that could have us all whacked out by the end of the night."

"You scared, Blood?" Pavielle asked. "I gotta tell you, Big Bro, yellow doesn't look right on you."

Scurrrrrr!

Gouch stopped the car in the middle of the road. In one swift motion he whipped around drawing one of his Girls. He pointed it in Pavielle's face and stared dead into his eyes.

"For as long as your asshole points to the ground don't chu ever mention me and scared in the same sentence, Homeboy." Gouch growled, his intimidating eyes staring into his brother's. "I've killed more men than you can count on both your fingers and toes. There isn't a nigga on this planet that I'm scared to bump heads with. This includes you."

"That's what I'm talking about; that's the Gucci I need on my team." Pavielle wore a serious expression. "When it's time to get active with this nigga Jesus, this is who I need by my side."

With that said, Gouch turned back around in his seat, threw the gear in drive and drove off.

"Fuck are we gonna do now?" Gouch asked. "We're running low on coke and we don't have a plug."

"I gotta couple of people I can hit up, so don't fret my boy." Pavielle patted his shoulder. "Our problems of today will be a thing of the past."

"I sure hope you're right."

"I am. Trust me." He took a pull from the L and passed it to Gouch.

SIXTEEN

A week later

Gouch executed the engine of the Hummer and hopped out. He took a quick scan of the area, adjusted The Girls on his waistline and made his way to the sidewalk. Pavielle had just stepped out of the beast and slammed the door shut. He and Gouch stood side by side staring up at the glowing sign of the marijuana clinic they were about to enter, 4/20. The name was catchy and made plenty sense since 4/20 was the national weed smokers' holiday. It gave all of the Pot Heads a good reason to smoke as if they needed one.

"Well, Gucci, let's see this man about this dog." Pavielle stepped forth and knocked on the black iron door. A moment later he heard a buzz and the door clicked opened. He pulled open the door and Gouch followed him inside. They took in their surroundings. There were various portraits of iconic characters and celebrities smoking weed. There were three aisles separated by glass shelves. Each shelf had a unique bong or smoking instrument. The rest of the shelves had scented candles, incense, burning oils, lighters and jugs of a special kind of liquid that could clean your piss. In the far left corner there were mix-tapes by every artist you could imagine and in the far right there were bootleg DVDs. Scattered throughout the store were racks of T-shirts with phrases about getting high or being high. Styles P's 'I Get High' played softy from the small speakers that hung from all four corners of the establishment. Pavielle and Gouch looked to their right and found a counter incased in bulletproof glass. On the walls were glass shelves that had large jars filled with marijuana nuggets with labels across them. The labels told the customers what kind of marijuana they had in stock: O.G Kush, Blue Ivy, Train Wreck, etc.

A short, portly woman came from behind the counter and protection of the bulletproof glass. She rocked a shaved head and had a body the shape of a small refrigerator. She wore glasses, a smock and jeans. At the small of her back was a Glock held in a Velcro strapped holster.

"Hi, how are ya fellas doing? I'm Tudy." She wiped her hands off on the smock and shook Pavielle and Gouch's hands. "I take it ya here ta see Furious."

"Indeed we are." Pavielle responded.

"Right dis way, Gentlemen." Tudy motioned for Pavielle and Gouch to follow her.

Tudy led Pavielle and Gouch down a corridor and through a storage space littered with boxes of paraphernalia. She stopped at the next door, which was thick, black and iron. There was a digital key-pad above the door knob. A surveillance camera was sat at the right high corner of the door and was pointed directly at the doorway. Tudy blocked Pavielle and Gouch's view of the key-pad with her back as she pressed the numeric code into the key-pad. The key-pad beeped and its red light turned green. Tudy turned the door knob and pushed her way inside.

Furious office was decorated like a Man Cave. There was a black leather couch on both sides of the room, a fully stocked bar at the far right corner and a '70 LED flat-screen attached to the north wall. At the south wall, Furious sat at a huge black wooden desk taking tokes of a joint the size of a fat man's thumb. His eyes were so low that you would have thought he'd fallen asleep in his chair. Furious was a high yellow nigga straight out of Kingston, Jamaica. He had little to no facial hair to speak of and his short hair was in twelve neat cornrows that barely touched the back of his neck. He was draped down in a royal blue Nike track suit and crisp royal blue and white Air Force Ones. An icy gold medallion hung against his chest and boasted the island of his birth place decorated in red, yellow, and green diamonds. His scrawny fingers had a gold ring on each one of them. The rings were unique in appearance and unusually big. The nail on the thumb of his right hand was about an inch long. He used it to split open blunts.

Furious was so engrossed in the boxing match playing out on the flat-screen that he didn't even notice Tudy come through the door. It wasn't until she knocked on the door that he took notice of her presence and the gentlemen she had with her.

"Furious, Mr. Hood and his brudda are here ta see ya." Tudy told him.

Furious lifted a finger and silenced Tudy. He closed his eyes and lay back in his chair. His lip quivered and he grunted, jerking violently. When he peeled his eyes open, a sexy young thang came up from his lap. She was banana yellow with freckles and had a scalp full of brown dread locks. She wiped her mouth with the back of her hand and licked her full lips.

"Clean up da mess ya made, Darling." Furious said, staring at the back of the young thang's head. She pulled open his desk drawer and snatched a couple of baby wipes from a plastic white box. She wiped Furious's junk down and tucked it back into his pants. She rose to her feet, pulling down her form fitting white dress. She then slipped on her oversized designer shades, grabbed her clutch, and sashayed to the door.

"Please, please, have a seat." Furious told Pavielle and Gouch, motioning a jeweled hand towards the chairs before his desk. "Can I interest you gentlemen in a drink or Chiba?" He touched the big red ceramic bowl on his desk that was filled with pretty green nuggets of weed. Its aroma was so strong that Pavielle was sure he was going to catch a contact from it.

"I'm good." Pavielle told him.

Furious looked to Gouch.

"I'm straight."

"Bumbaclot," Furious scowled, looking at the flat-screen watching the fighter he placed a million dollar bet on slam face first into the canvast. "Get up ya batty boy, mi gotta lotta cash riding on your ass!" he sighed and said to no one in particular, "Fucking Mayweather beats them everytime. Mi should learn by now." Shaking his head, he picked up the remote and turned the flat-screen off. He then lay back in his chair, focusing his attention on Pavielle as he took slow drags from the huge joint between his fingers. "So, Booby wot brings ya here?"

"Business."

"Hmmph," Furious nodded and massaged his chin. "Wot kinda business would ya be referring ta? Furious has his hands in a lotta tings, ya hear me?"

"Bitches."

"Oooooooh, Bitches." Furious said.

Pavielle nodded and said, "Is it all right for us to discuss them here?"

Furious took a deep breath and opened his arms wide. "Dee floor is open; speak your mind, Young Brudda."

Pavielle went on to tell Furious how many 'Bitches' he wanted and how much he was trying to pay for them. They haggled back and forth but eventually agreed upon $2,000 dollars above the price Pavielle originally wanted. With the deal made, Pavielle felt at ease. A smile surfaced as he felt the pressure lift from off his shoulders. He could finally get back to the money without any restrictions. Furious outstretched his hand. Pavielle's hand had almost grasped his when the telephone rang and he recoiled.

"Gimmie a minute," Furious held up a finger and snatched his cordless telephone up. He pressed talk and placed the telephone to his ear.

"Hello." Furious spoke into the telephone. His eyes shifted up from the desk and settled on Pavielle's. It was from this, that Pavielle knew that he was being discussed. Furious spun around in his chair, giving The Hood Brothers his back. They listened as he spoke in hush tones with whoever was on the other line of the telephone.

Something was wrong and Gouch could feel it in the air. He moved to draw his Girls and leave Furious's insides in his lap. Seeing this, Pavielle grasped his wrist and shot him a look that settled the beast stirring inside of him. He didn't want anything to pop off yet. He wanted to see exactly what the hell was going on.

"Peace." Furious disconnected the call and spun back around in his chair. He scratched his temple with the cordless telephone as he tried to figure out how he was going to come at Pavielle.

"What's the deal, Furious?"

"Brudda, it is with a heavy heart that I have to take that deal off of the table."

"What the fuck?" Pavielle said angrily. "Why?"

"You wanna know why? I'll tell you why?" Gouch spoke up, shooting daggers in Furious's direction. "Someone's working this puppet's strings."

"Is that true, Furious? Are you playing someone's bitch, nigga?"

Furious could feel the tension growing thicker in the room. So, while he was talking it out with Pavielle, he swiftly pressed a silent button located under his desk. The button glowed red and he slipped open his desk drawer. He dipped his hand inside and when it came back up it was gripping an Uzi.

"Mi, no one's bitch, you'd do betta watching ya tongue, boi." Furious scowled. "Mi have ties ta da mon ya severed ties wit. Him supply mi, him tell mi if I serve ya then him cut mi off."

"Ain't this about a bitch," Pavielle glanced at Gouch. "You're the sixth nigga I've been to this week that's cut me off on the strength of this fool! I mean, is there anyone that he doesn't have in pocket out this mothafucka?"

"Brudda, him got da sweetest coke. No one wants ta risk being cut off." Furious admitted.

Pavielle blew hard and brought his hands down his face.

"I can't do nothing but respect where you coming from, Furious." Pavielle told him. "I'm not tryna fuck up your paper."

Boom!

Tudy shot up from the trapped door behind Furious's desk, sweeping an AK-47 with a long ass banana clip from Pavielle to Gouch. Her finger was resting on the trigger and was ready to open a nigga's chest up.

"It's OK Tudy, me and da young brudda have came ta an undastanding." Furious raised a hand and Tudy reluctantly lowered her AK-47.

"I'm sorry about all this shit, Furious." Pavielle and Gouch rose to their feet.

"Mi too, mi sorry mi can't help ya." Furious outstretched his hand. "No hard feelings?"

"No hard feelings." He shook his hand.

"Tudy, I want cha ta give mi friends here a couple a grams of whateva they want, on da house." Furious told her.

"Nah, you don't have to do that, Furious." Pavielle waved him off.

"Please." Furious placed his hand to his chest. "Mi feel bad 'bout backing out of our deal. Mi would like for ya ta take someting wit cha."

"Furious, I…"

Furious raised a jeweled hand and cut Pavielle short.

"Young Brudda, please, mi won't accept no for an answer."

"Alright."

Tudy led Pavielle and Gouch out of Furious's office.

$$$

"Fuck am I going to do now?" Pavielle asked no one in particular as he and Gouch made their way towards the Hummer.

"There's no one else you can think of that'll probably put something in our hands?" Gouch inquired.

"Yeah, I could probably get my hands on some mediocre shit, but when the Heads think of Booby they think of a quality product." Pavielle relayed. "I want to keep it that way."

"Fuck it." Gouch went on to spit what was on his mind. "I can assemble a crew and we can start kicking in doors, robbing niggaz for their work and recycling it through our traps."

"Nah," Pavielle hopped into the front passenger seat, slamming the door shut. "The last thing we need is another beef; we already got our hands full with these fools from the other side. As of today all of the spots are shut down until we find another plug."

"You sure you wanna go through with this?" Gouch asked. "We stand to lose a lotta business."

"We'll get 'em back." Pavielle assured him. "They'll come running back once they hear I'm back open for business."

"Alright, if that's how you wanna play it." Gouch resurrected the Hummer and pulled off.

"The Trap God will smile down on us again, Gucci." Pavielle said, watching the streets breeze past him from the front passenger window. "I just know it."

SEVENTEEN

That night

When Ziggy crossed the threshold into The Bar Fly he noticed that the establishment was packed. His eyes scanned the many faces of the patrons until he found who he was looking for. The cat he was supposed to meet was sitting at the bar hunched over a glass of dark liquor. The man would occasionally glance up at the '30 flat-screen at the basketball game as he took casual sips of his drink. Ziggy loosened his tie and tugged on his collar to let his neck breathe. He mentally prepared himself then started for the fellow he was supposed to meet.

As soon as Ziggy's ass met the stool beside Pavielle, the bartender, old man Nigel approached, began popping the caps off a couple of Bud Wisers.

"What would ya like, Friend?" Nigel asked him pleasantly.

"Uh, how about a Rum and Coke?" Ziggy said.

"My man, coming right up," he bopped off two give the other patrons their beers and prepare Ziggy's drink.

Pavielle froze his glass at his lips as he was about to take a sip. He was staring up at the flat-screen when he spoke to Ziggy.

"You got my money?"

"Yep," Ziggy replied.

There was a moment of silence and then the young kingpin spoke again.

"Well, where the fuck is it?"

"Thanks." Ziggy said to Nigel, receiving his drink. He placed a fifty dollar bill on the bar top and slid it forth. "You can keep the change."

"Thank you." Nigel rang up the drink at the cash register. His eyes shifted from Pavielle to Ziggy. He knew that they had something going on, but it was none of his business so he moved on, mingling with the rest of the patrons.

"It's in trunk of my car." Ziggy leaned closer. "I had to take out a loan on a couple of my properties for that loot. My wife will probably leave me when she finds out."

"Fuck does that have to do with me?" Pavielle finally made eye contact.

"Are you kidding?" Ziggy frowned. "It's you who's putting the muscle on me for the bread. You and that young hoodlum, coming up to my office and terrorizing me and my daughter, that was uncalled for. If you really needed the money that bad I could..." Ziggy was cut short when Pavielle's hand shot down and grabbed his balls. He squeezed them so tight that Ziggy bit down on his bottom lip and tears ran from the corners of his eyes. Ziggy squirmed and gripped the edge of the bar. His testicles felt like they were about to explode in the palm of Pavielle's hand. Pavielle slipped his hand inside of Ziggy's suit's jacket. When he withdrew it he was holding his cell phone. Looking down at the screen, it was just as he thought, their conversation was being recorded. Pavielle's brow furrowed and he clenched his teeth, flexing the muscles in his jaws. He was so hot you could fry an egg on his forehead.

"Youz a dirty mothafucka, you know that, Ziggy?" Pavielle said. "I bet chu planned on taking this to The Boys and tell 'em that I'm extorting you, huh? Deceitful bastard…"

Smack!

Ziggy's head snapped to the right when Pavielle brought his jeweled hand across it. His ringed fingers left two small cuts on the side of Ziggy's face. Pavielle released his balls and he sighed with relief as he massaged them with both hands. Pavielle looked over his shoulder and motioned Gouch over. In a flash, his big brother was at the bar. He jammed his tool into Ziggy's side and whispered something into his ear. Together they left the bar with Pavielle bringing up the rear. Passing a table with a pitcher of beer left unattended, Pavielle dropped Ziggy's cell phone in it and went about his business.

Gouch and Pavielle stood to Ziggy left and right as he popped open the trunk. He did the combination on the briefcase and lifted the lid. Inside there were rows and rows of the new big face Benjamin Franklin bills. Pavielle closed the briefcase and removed it from the trunk. He turned to Ziggy, mad dogging him but never uttering a word. Ziggy squirmed under the intensity of his eyes. He felt like butter melting under the heat of his glare. Without warning, Pavielle smacked him upside the head. He assaulted his noodle with his open palm until his nostrils were flaring and he was heaving out of breath. Pavielle was steaming mad. He saw more small cuts opening on the side of Ziggy's face from his smacking him and looked to the rings on his fingers. The platinum and diamonds on the rings were speckled with blood. Pavielle pulled the frightened man into him, wiping his rings and hand on his button-down shirt.

"Bro, I'll slump this chump right now, just gimmie the nod." Gouch grabbed Ziggy by the back of the neck and pressed his tool to the back of his melon. He took a cautious look over his shoulders to make sure there weren't any witnesses about in case he laid his murder game down.

"Nah, that's alright." Pavielle said to Gouch, but never took his eyes off of Ziggy who couldn't even look him in the eyes he was so petrified. He was shaking like them bitches King of Diamonds. "Put cha hands on edge of the trunk, Nigga."

Ziggy looked to Pavielle with sad puppy dog eyes. "Pavielle, Man, please…"

He was silenced by another smack upside the head.

"Bitch, I don't got no sympathy for you! Now put cho dick tuggers on the edge, or call your wife to make them funeral arrangements!"

Ziggy hesitantly placed his hands on the trunk's edge. Pavielle nodded to Gouch and he pressed his steel to his temple.

Pavielle grabbed the trunk's lid and looked down at Ziggy.

"Move them bitches and my bro bro gone leave your thoughts in the street."

Slam!

The trunk slammed on Ziggy's hands, snapping bone and locking them in place. His eyes damn near shot out of his head. He nearly went hoarse from screaming so loudly. He fell to the side, hands still in the trunk, as he hollered for help and thrashed his legs around.

"Oh God, please somebody help! Help me!" he cried.

Slowly, the patrons began to emerge from the doorway of The Bar Fly.

Pavielle picked up the briefcase and followed his big brother back to the car. Gouch resurrected the vehicle and pulled off.

EIGHTEEN

She lay naked across the bed with her hand propped against her head, casually smoking a cigarette as she watched her sex partner attentively. He slid his muscular form from out of bed and slipped his thick legs into his Hanes boxer briefs. He then tied his rope thick dreads up with a blue bandana and rose to his feet, pulling a wife beater over his head.

"Where are you headed, Big Sexy?" she asked, dying for some more of that good shit between his legs. He'd beat her shit up good and left it stretched wide open. She'd come really hard and her pussy was wet and pulsating.

"I gotta get out in these streets and check these traps." He told her as he laced up his all blue Nike Cortez with the fat laces.

"What, you scared someone may try to clip you or something?"

"Nah, I don't think God created a mothafucka that stupid." Paybacc told her. "The name Paybacc means something out in these streets. Niggaz know that I'm willing to take it to a whole other level behind mine."

"Oooooooh, all that tough shit be turning a bitch on. That gangsta shit make my coochie wet, Daddy." She allowed her manicured hand to travel over the muscles of his left arm. It was well toned and had great definition. "Why don't chu gone and let momma get one more out chu before you roll out?"

"I've gotta take a rain check, Darling." Paybacc said. "I gotta tend to this business first. There are a number of days on the calendar for us to play."

"That's why I fuck with chu." She told him. "I love a thug ass nigga that's about his grip and slang good dick. You probably the only nigga that I've fucked with that has put cash over ass. Other fools want to lie up and play in this wet wet all day. I ain't mad at chu, Daddy, get yours. You just make sure that once you're finished out there in them streets that chu bring that ass back home to momma." She expelled white smoke and mashed her cigarette out into the ashtray.

"Youz a cool ass female, Lil Momma, respect," He gave her dap.

"Respect," She pulled him close by the back of his neck and kissed him hard and sloppily. Hearing her telephone, she pulled away leaving a length of saliva from her lips to his. She wiped her mouth with the back of her hand and looked at the caller ID. Seeing who it was she held a finger to her lips, signaling for Paybacc to be quiet.

"That's him?" Paybacc asked.

She nodded and cleared her throat, putting on her sexiest voice before answering the telephone.

"Hey, Daddy?" she cooed, twisting her manicured nail in the length of the cord while she talked. Paybacc leant closer and put his ear near the telephone, trying to listen to the conversation. About ten minutes later Paybacc's Fuck Buddy was hanging up the telephone.

"What did he say?" Paybacc inquired.

"He called to cancel our date tonight 'cause he has a lotta business he has to take care of, but promised to take me out tomorrow night." She informed Paybacc.

"Okilla, when y'all step out you be sure to let me know." Paybacc told her. "It's about time I closed the books on this Fuck-Boy."

Paybacc pulled a healthy roll of bills from his Dickies pocket. He peeled off a couple of Benjamin and threw them on the bed beside his conquest. "That's a lil something for you to play with."

"Aww, thank you, Boo Thang," She approached him on her knees on the bed. Clutching the money in her hand, she wrapped her arms around his neck and kissed him deeply.

"Let me get up outta here before my dick convinces me to stay." Paybacc cracked a smiled as he adjusted the hard-on in his pants.

"Stop fighting it, you know you can't resist this." She patted her shaved twat.

"You ain't never lied," Paybacc replied. "I'm outty 5,000, Lil Momma."

"See you later, Boo." She began counting the money she was given.

"Later, Poison."

Paybacc vanished through the doorway.

$$$

Chingo lay back in a chair with a smock tied around his neck to catch any loose hairs that may fall as his homeboy Cheese gave him an edge up.

"You know two of the homies got pinched last night." Cheese relayed as he busied himself with Chingo's facial hair. He was a tall, dark skinned cat with a Mohawk and an exotic design cut into both sides of his head.

"Who?" Chingo frowned.

"Set Tripp and Bad Lucc." Cheese told him.

"The fuck happened?"

"Shit, hustling. Set Tripp got popped with a zone and a burner and Bad Lucc with a quarter. I guess cuz really does have that shit."

"What?"

"Bad luck!"

"Damn!"

"This back and forth thing with the Twinkies is making it harder and harder to make moves out here." Cheese said. "Niggaz can't hustle how they used to with The Ones around 24/7. Pretty soon mothafuckaz is gone have to start looking for honest jobs and shit."

"Shit ain't gone go that far, at least not for us."

Cheese cut off the clippers and pulled up a chair.

"What chu got up your sleeve, Cuz? Whatever it is I know you're bringing your nigga along for the ride."

"All day, I gots ta look out for my brother." He dapped Cheese up.

"So, what's up?"

"I gotta plug on some H with some lovely prices. I know I can move that shit with no problem, 'cause the cats out here got work that's been stepped on so many times that they can't give it away. Niggaz are sitting on some straight bullshit and I'ma 'bout to capitalize on it. The shit I'm getting is fresh off the boat, ain't never been touched. Cuz, I can have shit on smash with this dope, I just need to dead this beef, 'cause it'll be too hard to move this shit with The Boys breathing down our necks."

"Chingo, you and I both know that this shit is not going to stop till that nigga Booby's casket drops."

"Not necessarily." Chingo told him. "If I could get Booby to take a sit-down, I'm sure I could convince him to put an end to this shit altogether."

"How you figure?" Cheese asked, as he lined up Chingo's mustache.

"Negotiate, my nigga," Chingo told him. "Shit, if I can sell these fiends soap and powder, I sho' nuff can sell a nigga a dream, nah what I'm saying?"

"I'm definitely picking up what chu sitting down, but how do you think Paybacc is going to feel about chu taking a meeting with Booby?" Cheese asked. "If I know cuz, he's not going to be feeling that at all."

"Maybe so, it's a shot in the dark but fuck it." Chingo shrugged. "I'm not just talking about the future of me and my family, but the future of all of the homies as well. Think about it. A few years from now we all could be sitting pretty and toasting to the good life, nah what I'm saying?"

"I'm sold, my nigga." Cheese removed the smock and brushed the hairs from around Chingo's neck. "But the homie is still the shot-caller of the set, so if he says no then it's a no go."

Chingo looked himself over in the mirror, inspecting his edge up.

"Tell me something Cheese," Chingo began, "have you always abided by the rules?"

"Hell naw, Cuz, I'ma rebel!" Cheese answered. "I do what the fuck I want!"

Chingo sat the mirror down and turned around to Cheese, smiling from ear to ear.

"Exactly," Chingo said.

"I respect your G, Cuz." Cheese told him.

"As I do yours," They gave one another dap.

$$$

Black Jesus sat behind the desk inside of his study, taking puffs of a Cuban Cigar. His brown eyes were casted down on a portrait of him and Gangsta when they were young. They were wearing Dickie suits and bandanas were tied around their heads. Black Jesus was posing with twin Magnum revolvers while Gangsta was holding an AK-47. Back then they were two crazy kids living the life and trying to earn a rep. All they cared about then was status, money, women and their sets. Everything else paled in comparison. A smirk emerged on Black Jesus' face as he reminisced about his oldest and dearest friend. He felt stinging in his eyes and they began to mist. Black Jesus blinked back his tears and collected himself. It wasn't that he was too macho to cry. It was that his friend had always said that in his passing he wanted blood to be shed, not tears.

"Mr. Arturo." A feminine voice called from the doorway and stole Black Jesus' attention. His eyes shifted in the direction the voice came and found his maid, Marisol.

Black Jesus sat the portrait down on his desk and mashed his Cuban Cigar out in the ashtray.

"Yes," Black Jesus answered and cleared his throat.

"Mr. Bebo Sims is here to see you." Marisol stated.

"Send him right in."Black Jesus told her, before pouring up a glass of very expensive Cognac. No sooner than he'd corked the glass bottle containing the dark liquor and sat it down, Bebo came strolling into his study. Black Jesus took a sip of his drink and motioned for his guest to have a seat.

"Mr. Sims, could I interest you in a drink of your choice?" Black Jesus asked.

"No, thank you." Bebo answered. "I'd much rather discuss business."

"Right," Black Jesus sat the glass of Cognac down. "There are three people I need taken care of."

"Three, huh?" Bebo asked, withdrawing a cigarette from a wrinkled pack of Newport shorts. He held the cigarette up so that Black Jesus could see it. "You mind?"

"Please." Black Jesus responded.

Bebo took the time to fire up the cigarette before continuing, "A threesome is going to be expensive. My guys don't work for short paper."

"Money isn't a problem for me, I assure you."

"Which is why I'm even entertaining this conversation."

"What's your rate?"

Bebo took the cigarette from his mouth and licked his lips as he thought on it.

"Gimmie a hundred and fifty," Bebo told him. "That's thousand, not hundred."

"Got it."

"The retainer's fee is half that, up front."

"Not a problem."

"Now, what does this trio look like?"

Black Jesus slid a manila envelope before Bebo. The big man opened the manila envelope and pulled out three photographs. The photographs were of a man, a woman and new born baby. Seeing the baby took Bebo by surprise. He looked up to Black Jesus.

"One of them is of a new born baby."

"Yes, is that gonna be a problem?"

Bebo blew hard and looked over the photographs again.

"No," Bebo looked back up to Black Jesus. "Long as you can foot the bill everything's a go."

"Great."

"You got anything for my guys to go on?"

"The address is on the back of the photograph of the gentleman."

"Got any names to match with these faces?"

"Yes." Black Jesus answered. "The names are on the backs of the photos as well."

Bebo turned the photographs over and laid them flat on the desk. He read the name on each of the photographs: Pavielle, Vayda and Nasheed.

NINETEEN

A couple of nights later

Paybacc, Steel and Shadow sat around the kitchen table loading the last of the slugs into their weapons. They had a blunt in rotation and sipped dark liquor as they went about the task. Not even ten minutes ago, Paybacc had gotten a call from Poison letting him know that she was about to head out for a night on the town with Pavielle. Once she'd texted Paybacc the address of the location, he didn't waste any time calling up his blood thirsty pups, Steel and Shadow. They jumped at the chance to put in work alongside their mentor.

The threesome had finished loading their weapons and rose to their feet. Paybacc took one last pull from the L before he mashed what was left of it out into the ashtray. Paybacc and his pups were headed for the front door when they heard someone knock on it. Paybac stole a glance through the peephole. He then unlocked and unchained the door, snatching it open. Chingo crossed the threshold and pulled the hood from his head. Paybacc closed the door behind him.

"What's cracking, Loco? We were just on our way out." Paybacc informed him.

"I gotta way to resolve this thing with them niggaz from the other side." Chingo told him.

"I do to, and its name is MAC-10." Paybac held up his weapon.

"Nah, if we do this my way there won't be any bloodshed."

"What're you suggesting, a truce?" Paybacc asked with narrowed eyes.

"Yeah," Chingo nodded, "Something like that."

"I don't know about you, but I left that truce in '92." Paybac admitted. "This thing we got going doesn't end until that mothafucka and his brother are no longer with us. You feel me?"

"I got this plug on this Dog Food," Chingo tried another angle. "The shit is pure and I can get it at a cool ass price. I know I can move this shit," he clapped his hands for emphasis. "But I need for this killing to stop so I can get this shit off the ground. I'm talking big bucks, Cuz, me and you could be millionaires in the next year."

"I'm already a millionaire, Chingo." Paybacc confessed. "Fuck the money, it ain't about the money. It's about making these slobs bleed for touching our brothas. I wouldn't be able to sleep at night knowing I done brokered a truce with the enemy. Fuck them niggaz."

"You aren't hearing me."

"I heard you, Chingo. The dead homies heard you, too." Paybacc assured him. "And right now they're turning over in their graves 'cause they can't believe that you're standing before me right now sounding like a fucking punk."

Chingo mad dogged Paybacc and balled his fists tight. He wanted to draw steel and put some hot shit through his brain, but he was sure the O.G would have took him off his feet before he could clear his banger from his waistline."

"I think we're done here." Paybacc said.

"Yeah, we're done." Chingo replied with attitude.

"All right then, we're up." Paybacc stashed the MAC-10 on his person and snatched the front door open. He, Steel, and Shadow made their exit.

$$$

Gouch played the role of chauffer while Pavielle and Poison rode in the backseat. The two of them partook in a fat blunt and chatted during the ride. Twice, their conversation was interrupted by Poison answering text messages. Though this irritated Pavielle, he kept his feelings in check. He was enjoying her company and didn't want the night to take a turn for the worse.

"I know that bet not be no other nigga you're talking to." Pavielle tried to steal a peek at Poison's cell phone but she hurriedly sent a text message and dropped it into her designer bag. She turned back around wearing a smile and applying MAC lip-gloss to her lips.

"Nope, you're the only one for me, Boo Boo." She kissed Pavielle on the side of his face.

"That's right, run that game, Girl." He passed her the blunt.

"That wasn't game that was real spit." She took a couple puffs.

"I know game when I hear it."

"We're here." Gouch announced as he executed the engine.

Poison looked out of the backseat window and found a two story house. The house was dark save for the light illuminating over the porch.

"What's this? I thought we were going gambling." She asked Pavielle.

"This is the gambling spot." Pavielle assured her. Big Mel gotta casino setup in his basement. Craps, cards, slot machines, he got some of everything down there. It's like the ghetto Los Vegas. The best thing is that if you win you don't have to pay taxes on any of the loot. All the big time money getters come and try their luck here."

"Oh OK, that's what's up, then."

"Come on; let's see what's up in here." Pavielle took Poison by the hand and helped her out of the Hummer.

$$$

Paybacc sat low in the driver seat of the Nissan Pathfinder as he captained it through the streets. On board was Steel and Shadow riding with their compact machineguns in their laps. The gruesome threesome kept their eyes on the streets and everyone on them. Operation Kill Booby Loco was in full effect.

The truck was silent being that each individual man was occupied with his own thoughts. The chirping of a cell phone with a new text message stole Shadow and Steel's attention. They looked to Paybacc who was taking his cell phone from his hip. Paybacc's eyes went back and forth from the windshield to the screen of the cell phone as he read the message.

WE'RE LEAVIN NOW!

"OKILLA"

Paybacc texted back and slipped his cell back into his pocket.

"Yo, this is it right here." Steel said of the spot they were to catch Pavielle slipping.

"We're right on time." Paybacc smirked.

Paybacc pulled alongside the curb underneath the shade of a tree where they wouldn't be seen. The three men patiently watched the house that their target was to emerge from. Moments later, the shadows surrounding the house began to stir, causing Paybacc and Shadow to look alive. They spotted Pavielle, Gouch, and Poison making their way through the front yard.

"That's them Cuz, we're on." Shadow said, masking up. He glanced to the backseat. "Come on, Steel."

Steel and Shadow pulled their ski-masks down over their faces to conceal their identities. They hopped out of the Path Finder and closed the doors, careful not to make a sound. Slowly, they moved in on an unsuspecting Pavielle and Gouch, fingers ready to squeeze the triggers tighter than their true loves. By the time Pavielle and Gouch stepped out onto the sidewalk, Shadow and Steel had emerged from the shadows of the darkened block. They'd just lifted their machineguns and were about to fire when Gouch spotted them from the corner of his eye.

With lightning fast reflexes, Gouch kicked Poison back into the yard and on to the lawn. He then tackled Pavielle to the ground and whipped out his Girls, aiming them at the would-be killers. Gouch squeezed off the handguns rapidly, holes exploded out of Shadow and Steel's backs. Agony registered on their faces before they fell out on the sidewalk, staining the concrete with their blood.

Gouch lie on top of Pavielle waving his Girls back and forth. His head whipped around in all directions making sure there weren't any more killers coming for him and his brethren. Figuring that they were safe and sound, Gouch got to his feet and stashed his Girls on his waistline. Pavielle scooped his cane up into his mitt and Gouch pulled him to his feet. Poison ran out of the yard and threw her arms around him.

"You, all right?" Gouch asked Pavielle.

"I'm straight." Pavielle replied. He looked to Poison. "You good, Momma?"

She nodded yes.

"Did you see who it was?" Pavielle asked Gouch.

A groan of pain drew Pavielle and Gouch's attention to their left. They found one of their would-be killers squirming and bleeding like a stuck pig. They hastily approached him. Gouch yanked the ski-mask from his face and revealed his identity.

"Shadow; and I bet this fuck-nigga is Steel." Pavielle nudged the body lying beside Shadow with his cane. He then yanked the ski-mask from his head. Steel's eyes were bulging and his mouth was wide open. He wore The Face of Death. "Well, can you believe it? I'm better than them hoes at The Psychic Friends Network."

"G-momma used to go to church with these fools grand momma. Do you believe this shit, Man?" Gouch pressed his sneaker into Shadow's wounded torso, causing him to scream.

"Well, that didn't stop 'em from tryna air hole our black asses, now did it?"

Pavielle and Gouch were engrossed in their conversation that they didn't see Shadow scooping the compact machinegun into his crimson stained hand. Shadow went to lift the lethal weapon and fire shot through his wrist. His eyes shifted to Gouch. His nostrils were flaring and he was pointing one of his Girls dead at his face. Shadow's lips went to spit an insult and Gouch exercised his trigger-finger.

Boc! Boc! Boc! Boc! Boc! Boc!

The top of Shadow's head and his bottom jaw came apart. His form crashed to the sidewalk and he released his last breath. His soul shot into an afterlife where there are dancing demons and sweltering temperatures. Gouch took the time to admire his handiwork before tapping Pavielle and starting towards the Hummer. They'd just reached the Hummer when a ear piercing sound ripped through the air…

Urrrrk!

The Nissan Pathfinder skidded to a stop and Paybacc leaned over the front passenger seat, gripping his compact machinegun. His face twisted and he growled angrily as he pulled the trigger. The MAC-10 vibrated in his palm as he hugged its trigger. The weapon spat rapidly and without remorse. The Kia Optima that Pavielle, Poison and Gouch had just taken cover behind, slightly rocked as it was riddled with holes and its windows exploded. Realizing that he'd missed his targets, Paybacc threw the door open and hopped out of the Pathfinder. With determionation and vengeance on his mind, he jogged from around the Pathfinder. He was about to step upon the curb and lay down some gunplay, when he heard the very familiar chirp of police crusier sirens. Paybacc stopped in his tracks and looked up the block. As sure as his ass was tall, buff and black there were two police cruisers approaching from a block away.

"Shit!" Paybacc punched the back of the Pathfinder, hating that he couldn't put his beef to bed. He hopped back behind the wheel of the Pathfinder and sped off. Once Paybacc had vanished, Pavielle, Poison and Gouch ducked back inside of Big Mel's yard. They lay low inside of his basement until the police dispersed and then they took their leave.

TWENTY

Paybacc sat in the backseat of a Pontiac Grand Prix staring out of the back window and opening and closing the top of a Zippo lighter. He watched as two of the homies rolled down the windows of the Pathfinder and drenched its dashboard and seats with gasoline. Paybacc loved the truck but it was time that he parted ways with it. Truthfully, he should have been done got rid of it. He had busted on so many Bloods out of it that he knew that it was as hot as a fire cracker by now. It wasn't any doubt in his mind that the truck was on the police as well as his enemies' radar. The Pathfinder had to go and it was with a heavy heart he had to say, Von Voyage.

The night's botched hit had really gotten under Paybacc's skin. He had gotten so close to Pavielle that he could have spit on him, but he had missed his chance. He wished he could have resurrected Steel and Shadow from the dead just so he could kill them again. He couldn't believe that they'd fucked up the murder. He had everything laid out for them. Pavielle's life was right there for the taking, they just had to grab it. It was quite easy. All they had to do was get close enough to guarantee a kill-shot and pull the trigger. It was so simple to Paybacc. So he couldn't understand for the life of him why Pavielle's people weren't making funeral arrangements for him right this minute.

"Fuck, Cuz!" Paybacc punched the back of the front passenger seat. He was heated with not only Steel and Shadow, but himself. He was to blaim also. He had to bare some of the weight. He knew more than anyone else what he had riding on the execution of Pavielle, which was why he shouldn't have let a couple of novices helm the responsibility. Paybacc shouldn't have entrusted the pups with the big dog's job. If he would have handled things himself there would have been a visual and candle light ceremony going on somewhere inside of the 20's in the memory of one, Booby Loco.

Feeling that he was a failure and deserving of punishment, Paybacc drew a flame with the Zippo lighter and held his palm over it. The flame danced beneath his hand, causing it to sizzle. Paybacc's face twitched and he clenched his teeth. He faught back the pain stemming from the fire cooking his flesh. It wasn't until the smell of his burning skin crept up his nostrils that he snapped the Zippo lighter closed. He looked at the area of his palm that he held the flame of the lighter under and saw that it had shriveled like a dried prune. Paybacc made his hand into a fist and laid it in his lap. As soon as he rested his dreads against the headrest a sudden noise made him look alive.

Froooooosh!

Boooom!

Paybacc's neck snapped around to where he heard the explosion. From the window he saw the burning Pathfinder and the homies running in his direction, their silhouettes shone on the ground.The homies hopped back into the Pontiac Grand Prix and pulled away from the fire.

"You taking it to the house, Paybacc?" The homie asked from behind the wheel.

"Yeah, Cuz, shoot me to the crib." Paybacc said, keeping his eyes on his cell phone's screen as he scrolled through the listed contacts. Once he located the number he was looking for, he tapped the dial sign and pressed the cell to his ear.

$$$

Chingo was hunched over a plate of cocaine snorting a line with a rolled up $100 dollar bill. Once he'd finished the line he threw his head back and pinched his nose. He did this to stop from sneezing and wasting the drug. Chingo wiped his nose with the back of his hand. He blinked his glassy eyes and looked about. He damn near jumped out of his skin when he saw Cheese coming from out of the bathroom, zipping up his jeans. He'd forgotten that he'd called him over to get high.

Chingo took a sip from a clear plastic cup of Hennessy. He swirled the liquor around in the cup as he watched Cheese snort a line from off the plate. Paybacc had gotten Chingo so heated that he couldn't wait to get to his low key apartment in West L.A. As soon as he walked through the door, he grabbed an ounce of that pure and a couple of playing cards. Once Chingo had chopped up and smoothed out the cocaine, he scrolled through the contacts in his cell phone to find a get-high buddy. When he came across Cheese's name, he didn't waste any time putting a call through to his closest comrade. He fucked with Cheese hard body. He was one of the few homies that he kicked it with. They were just alike in many ways.

"I told you that fool wasn't going to feel your proposal." Cheese thumbed his nose and tried to pass the rolled up bill to Chingo.

"I'm good, Cuz," Chingo told him. "But yeah, Man, that cock sucker had me so hot I wanted to tag his toe right then and there. I started to too, but that mothafucka had that thang on 'em. Not to mention if I was to take him off his feet it would have caused a rift in the set. You know a lotta niggaz from the hood got love for cuz."

"True," Cheese poured up a cup of Hennessy. "But there's a lotta homies that got love for you, too."

"I'm already knowing," Chingo took a sip from his cup.

"So what chu gone do, Cuz, let this lil' war keep going until it fizzles out?"

"Fuck nah, I'm not letting this shit stun the growth of my paper." He shot the notion down. "I just gotta go at this situation from a different angle, know what I'm talking about?"

"Enlighten me." Cheese took a sip of Hennessy.

A smile stretched across Chingo's face as he held up the Zip-loc bag of cocaine.

"That'll be his third strike." He informed him. "He'll never see daylight again."

"Yep, and he'll be outta my hair." Chingo claimed. "Then all I have to do is talk this nigga Booby into letting bygones be bygones."

"That's one beautiful mind you've got there, Chingo." Cheese grinned.

"To millionaire status," Chingo held up his plastic cup.

"To millionaire status," he held up his plastic cup.

The Crips toasted and sipped their drinks.

Just then, Chingo's cell phone rung and he looked at its screen. A shit eating grin formed on his face and he looked to

Cheese, showing him who the caller was. Cheese smiled and nodded his head. Chingo answered the cell phone.

"Paybacc, what's up with it, Cuz?" A big ass smiled stretched across that nigga'z face.

$$$

Paybacc sat hunched over the coffee table greasing his burn with ointment. Once he was done he wrapped his hand in gauze and medical-tape. He picked up a bottle of Jack Daniel's and was about to pour up a shot. Suddenly, he stopped and thought for a second. Coming to a conclusion, he shrugged, smacked the glass off the coffee table, and took the Jack to the dome. Hearing a knock at the door, Paybacc sat the bottle of Jack down and wiped his mouth with the back of his hand. He picked the Desert Eagle up from the coffee table and stood to his feet. He approached the door cautiously and peered through the peephole. After identifying who it was on the other side, he unchained and unlocked the door. Payabacc snatched open the door and allowed Chingo inside. Chingo plopped down on the La-Z-Boy reclining chair while Paybacc copped a seat on the arm of the couch.

"So, what's up, Cuz? What's the big emergency?"

"Steel and Shadow got their dicks left in the dirt."

Chingo closed his eyes and shook his head. He hated to hear that two more of the homies had gotten twisted. This was exactly what he didn't want. If Paybacc would have listened to him they probably could have saved their lives, but he had to be so goddamn stubborn and have things his way. Now they had two more casualties to add to the body count.

"What happened?"

"You know the rules, Cuz, we don't discuss bodies." Paybacc told him. "Murder is a touchy subject."

"Right," Chingo thought on it. "You know this shit could have possibly been avoided, right?"

Paybacc rolled his eyes and blew hard.

"Here we go again!"

"You mothafucking right, Cuz," Chingo caught an attitude. "If we would have gone at this shit my way, Steel and Shadow could still be alive and our pockets could be a lot fatter."

"Mayabe so, but chu forget one lil' thing, Chingo," Payabcc held up a crooked finger.

"What's that?"

"I'm the captain of this here ship, and I'm running this shit to the beat of my own drum. And any homeboy that ain't with it can jump ship and take a chance at the sink or swim game, ya feel me?" Paybacc's dark eyes bored into Chingo's. A moment of silence passed between them then Chingo's cell phone rung. He answered the cell phone, listened to what the caller had to say, and hung up. He then got to his feet, slipping the cell phone into his pocket.

"That's the money calling, Loc, I gotta make my outro." He told Paybacc.

Chingo and Paybacc slapped hands and embraced. When they broke the show of love, Paybacc held him at arms length.

"Why did I get the distinct feeling that you was hovering a knife near my back just now?"Paybacc asked seriously.

Chingo narrowed his eyes at him and tilted his head to the side.

Paybacc shrugged, staring him dead in his eyes. "He, who betrays his brother, shall not find peace; not even in Death."

Chingo yanked away from him, pointing a finger in his face.

"You're fucked up, Man, you know that? You're fucked up!"

Chingo opened the front door and made his exit. Paybacc watched him leave then peered through the blinds. Once he saw his car leave the parking lot, he returned to his post on the couch, drinking himself into a stupor.

$$$

Chingo hopped behind the wheel of his ride and resurrected the engine. He waited until Cheese was perched in the front passenger seat and then he pulled off.

"You put that shit in there?" Chingo inquired.

"Yep," Cheese nodded. "I hid it inside the glove-box."

"Cool." Chingo said. "Now we just gotta wait for his ass to leave tomorrow and make that call."

"Yeah, niggaz 'bout to be on," Cheese touched fists with Chingo.

Chingo cranked up the volume on Rick Ross's 'Nobody' and mashed the gas pedal. The Monte Carlo took off gunning through stop-signs and red lights.

TWENTY ONE

After dropping Poison off at home and making her promise to keep her mouth shut, The Hood Brothers found themselves on the road home. This was the second attempt on Pavielle's life and again he'd made it by the skin of his ass. Every time he found himself on Death's doorstep, The Grim Reaper would slam the door in his face. Pavielle knew that there wasn't anything short of a miracle keeping him from sitting at the Lord's feet. He couldn't help but to believe his Loved Ones in the heavens above were looking out for him. How else could he make sense of his being alive? In his mind he should have been gone, especially with all of the dirt he'd done throughout his life.

Steel and Shadow seemed to have appeared out of thin air with machineguns. If it wasn't for Gouch being on point, Pavielle was sure he wouldn't have been alive to see another sunset. He understood the importance of having someone to watch your back. He was glad that Gouch was a willing tag along whenever he decided to step out in the streets. As long as he had the support of his big brother and his stalwart soldiers, Pavielle was sure he'd conquer whatever obstacle that stood in his way. He was sure of that if he wasn't of anything else.

Pavielle rolled in the front passenger seat of the Hummer caressing the gold rosary that hung from his neck with his thumb as he thought about the night's botched hit. The gears of his mind turned and theories manifested. An epiphany ripped through his mental and caused him to sit up in his seat. Clearing his throat, he turned to Gouch.

"Turn around."

Gouch turned the volume down on the stereo and said, "Say what?"

"Turn this bitch around!" Pavielle spoke up.

Urrrrrrrk!

Gouch whipped the sexy red machine around and sped off back in the direction he'd come from. Once he reached his destination, he pulled alongside the curb, threw the gear in park and looked to Pavielle.

"What's up?" he asked, curiously.

"I'll be right back, keep this mothafucka running." Pavielle slammed the door shut and hurried along as fast as he could with his cane.

Pavielle stepped upon the porch of a familiar house and rang the doorbell. A second later, a sexy young thing stole a peek through the window from between the blinds. She then unlocked and opened the door.

"Hey, Boo, you forgot something?"

"Yeah, I forgot to give you these."

Boc! Boc! Boc! Boc!

Poison dropped where she stood with her body lying half way out of the door. The black holes in her form ran red with blood and seeped between the wooden floorboards of the porch. She gurgled on blood while staring up at Pavielle accusingly. She grasped his pants leg and he yanked it back.

"Old snake ass bitch; I should have seen you slithering my way!" Pavielle sneered. He pointed his banger at Poison's face and let off round after round, until the top of his weapon reclined and expelled white smoke. Pavielle pressed a button on his weapon that restored it back to its normal state. He ducked off into the house and returned moments later with Poison's cell phone. He scrolled through her text messages as he hustled down the steps.

Pavielle snatched open the door and hopped back into the front passenger seat. Gouch pulled away from the curb and drove off as if they hadn't just left the scene of a gruesome murder.

"You got cho flag?" Pavielle asked.

Gouch nodded. He pulled a red bandana from his back pocket and passed it to Pavielle. Carefully, the youngest of The Hood Brothers, wiped his finger prints off of the murder weapon and laid it on his lap.

"Stop right here so I can toss this." Pavielle pointed to an upcoming gutter. Gouch stopped the Hummer beside the curb and Pavielle opened the door. He gave the murder weapon one more good wipe down before ditching it in the gutter. He then slammed the door shut and the Hummer pulled off.

"What was all of that about?" Gouch asked, looking from the windshield to Pavielle, waiting for an answer.

"Bitch set me up." Pavielle answered. "Paybacc put Poison on me, she texted him the address to Big Mel's spot. Look," he showed Gouch the text in Poison's cell phone that she sent Paybacc. "It took a hot minute for me to piece it together, but in the end it all made sense."

"Shit, Man, you can't trust nobody." Gouch realized.

"You're goddamn right." Pavielle agreed. "From now on I'm looking at everybody as a suspect."

Pavielle tossed Poison's cell phone out of the window of the speeding Hummer.

TWENTY TWO

The net day

Paybacc had called Poison for what he figured was the millionth time and she hadn't answered. For every time he called, a million thoughts ripped through his brain. He came up with several different reasons why she hadn't answered his calls and neither one of them were good. They all lead back to Pavielle finding out she was his spy and blowing her brain up through the top of her skull. Paybacc hated to think that it went down that way but it was more than likely that it had occured. He couldn't shake the feeling that Poison was dead. He could feel it in his gut. Something told him that she was lying on a slab in the morgue about to have her autopsy performed.

Paybacc's mental assaulted him with images of Poison stretched out with two in her thinking cap, slumped on the couch with her throat slit from ear to ear, and sitting in her car with a strangle line around her neck. White flashes exploded inside of Paybacc's head; each one showing Poison lying murdered in a gory way. Having had enough of his imaginations torture, Paybacc rolled out of the bed and got dressed. After throwing his dreads in a blue band and securing his Desert Eagle on his waistline, he snatched up his keys and mobbed to the front door. He was on his way to Poison's house to see what the fuck was going on.

Paybacc hustled down the steps and hopped behind the wheel of his Chrysler 200. He slammed the door shut and resurrected the engine. He adjusted the rearview mirror and pulled off. He was none the wiser to violet '95 Honda Civic tailing him.

$$$

Paybacc had just turned onto Poison's block when he notices a host of police cruisers and a coroner's van crowding the front of her place. He allowed his Chryler 200 to coast along as he rode past Poison's house. Gripping the steering wheel, he looked out of the front passenger window and saw a body under a blood stained white sheet being rolled out of the yard. Several people were gathered around watching the coroners in action. Amongst them was a crack head by the name of Fast Talking Eddie. Paybacc remembered him from the last time he'd visited Poison, he'd paid him to clean the windows and rimz of his ride. He'd done a piss poor job, but Paybacc had tipped him a $20 dollar bill anyway just so he'd shut the fuck up. Paybacc whistled out of the window and Eddie turned around. Eddie peered inside of the Chrysler and when he saw Paybacc he broke out into a smile, boasting all four of his rottening teeth. He threw up a hand and Paybacc motioned him over. Paybacc pulled the Chrysler 200 alongside the curb. He looked over his shoulder and saw Eddie jogging in his direction. Hurriedly, he snatched open the door and hopped into the front passenger seat.

"What's up, Boss Hog? How're you doing? How have you been?" Eddie's mouth shot off like an AK-47. "Let me hit this windshield and these rimz for you, Baby. I promise I'll be quick; I just need a couple of dollars. Look out for yo people one time."

"I got fifty for you, Ed." Paybacc held up a folded $50 dollar bill. Seeing the fifty bucks caused Eddie's eyes to bulge. He licked his dry, chapped lips and went to grab the money, but Paybacc snatched it away. "If you can tell me who that was they rolled up outta there."

"Jamie." Eddie gave him Poison's government name. "I stopped by here this morning 'cause she was gone let me paint her living room for a couple of dollars, and when I gets here she's lying on the porch, flat-lined. Some wicked sum bitch shot her four times in the chest and I don't know how many times in the face." He shook his head as if to say it was a crying shame. "I couldn't even tell it was her until I seen those tattoos of hers, crying shame, Man. That poor girl ain't never done nothing to nobody. I'll tell you, Boss Hog, the evil that men do."

"Ain't nobody speaking up on who left the body?"

"Boss Hog, folks don't know nothing," Eddie told him. "All they heard were shots in the middle of the night. But shit, that the same as every other night. Hell, we're in the heart of the ghetto."

"Right," Paybacc gave Eddie the $50 dollar bill. He watched as he slipped on a pair of glasses and held the $50 dollar bill up to the sun, checking its authenticity. Once Eddie saw that the money was authentic, he stuffed it into his pocket, and removed his glasses. After tucking the specs inside of the pocket of his windbreaker, he turned to Paybacc.

"Look here, Boss Hog, why don't you gone 'head and let me hit this windshield and them rimz for you for five extra dollars? Fuck it, make it ten and I'll wash this sum bitch for you. I'll have this mothafucka shining like new money."

Paybacc chuckled and said, "I'll have to take a rain check, Fam. I gotta lotta shit I gotta do."

"Sho' ya right. Well, let me…" that was as far as Eddie got before the doors of the Chrysler were snatched open and he and Paybacc were yanked out of their seats. Two cops roughly handled them, slamming them to the hood of the car and slapping the cuffs on them.

"Yo, Man, what the fuck is this shit about?" Paybacc asked as he and Eddie were deposited into the back of a police cruiser. The police officers ignored them and headed back to the Chrysler. Paybacc watched as they combed through every nook and cranny of the vehicle. His heart pounded and he silently prayed that they didn't find the Desert Eagle he had tucked away. He'd hidden it inside of the stash spot, but the police weren't dummies. They were well informed on the stash places that niggaz had installed in their whips.

"Eddie, you didn't get into my shit dirty, did you?"

"Nah, Boss Hog, I'm clean."

Good, Paybacc thought. There weren't any drugs in the car so as long as The Boys didn't find the heater he was Good Money. Paybacc looked over his shoulder out of the back window. He watched as a violet Honda Civic sped down the block in reverse and whip around. He knew exactly who the car belonged to from the license plates, but he wondered what the fuck they were doing there. When Paybacc turned back around his brow furrowed. One of the police officers was heading in his direction. He seemed to be moving in slow motion, carrying an ounce of cocaine in his mitt. A smile was plastered on his face as he tilted the dark shades down and gave Paybacc a look. Seeing the expression on the officer's face made Payabcc think about the interrogation room scene in Menace II Society with Bill Dukes 'Now, you know you done fucked up, don't you?' Paybacc closed his eyes and leaned his head back against the seat. He'd been setup.

$$$

Chingo was kneeled before the back rim of his Monte Carlo spraying it with chrome cleaner and wiping it down. Once he polished the five star rims to a finish, he looked himself over in it. Satifised with the job, he stood erect and placed the items inside of his trunk. As soon as he slammed the trunk closed a violet Honda Accord pulled up and parked beside him.

The driver side door came open and Cheese hopped out, boasting all thirty two. The two men approached each other slapping hands and embracing.

"Uncle C," Cheese's son, JoJo, hopped out of the car and came running up.

"What's up, Lil' Nigga?" Chingo dapped him up.

"Ain't nothing, just chilling with my Dad."

"That's what's up."

"Man, that's a wavy ass chain you got on." JoJo admired the icy gold T.L.B a.k.a Tiny Loc Bastards chain dangling from his neck.

"You like this, huh?" Chingo looked down at the chain.

"Yeah, that's fly."

"Well, it's yours now."

"Really?" A smile stretched across JoJo's face.

"Yep, there you go." Chingo slipped the chain over JoJo's neck. "That's all you, Baby Boy."

"Wow, thanks, Uncle C." JoJo slapped hands with Chingo and embraced him.

Chingo reached into his pocket and pulled out some change. He shifted through the change picking out a couple of quarters.

"Nephew, why don't chu gone and play the arcade in the liquor store and gimmie and ya Pops a minute to chop it up."

"OK."

Chingo dropped the quarters into JoJo's hand and he dashed towards the liquor store. Cheese and Chingo watched him go, wearing smiles on their faces.

"Tell me something good, Loco." Chingo turned back around to Cheese.

"Got 'em coach," Cheese smiled, rubbing his hands together.

"For real?"

"Straight drop," Cheese assured him. "The Boys grappled him up."

"Cuz finished then, least he's got his life though."

"Straight up, 'cause it could have been worse, niggaz showed mercy."

Chingo nodded and said, "Now, it's time to get the ball rolling on this other thing."

"Man, I don't know how you gone pull this off without nobody getting hurt."

"Aye, you gotta crack a couple of eggs to make an omlette."

"True dat," Cheese dapped him up.

$$$

The police let Fast talking Eddie walk but they held fast to Paybacc. He was booked and placed into a holding cell with six other low lifes. The pod was occupied by cats from all walks of life. You had your pimps, hustlers, gangsters and cap peelers. Paybacc didn't waste anytime establishing his male dominance. He let niggaz know that he was the Alpha Male off top.

They got their first lesson on whom not to fuck with when a young degenerate tried Paybacc for his sack lunch. Paybacc kicked the youth in the balls and chopped him in the throat. The nigga fell to the floor gasping for air and holding his neck with both hands. Afterwards, Paybacc emptied the contents of his lunch out of the brown paper bag and into the toilet. He then flushed it down just to make a point.

Paybacc snatched the telephone from off the hook and punched in a number. He listened to the line ring as he watched the youth bawl on the floor in agony. He shook his head thinking of how stupid the kid was for testing his gangsta. Someone answered on the third ring and Paybacc focused his attention on the call at hand.

"Baby Girl?" he spoke into the receiver.

"Daddy?"

"Yeah, this me." Paybacc told Zora. "Listen, I need you to post my bail."

"What happened are you, OK?"

"I'm fine, Baby Girl. I'll explain everything later, but right now I need you to get me up outta here."

"How much is it?"

"It's 10 percent, so, uh, $2,000 grips." Paybacc told her. "I'll give it back to you once I get outta this hell."

"That's all right, Daddy, you blessed me with more than enough." Zora said. "I'm on my way to see about getting you out now, OK?"

"OKilla."

"I love you."

"I love you too, Baby Girl."

Paybacc hung the telephone up. He then kicked the kid on the floor and sat on the bench. He fished an orange out of the kid's brown paper bag and began to peel it. Zora was about to post his bail so he'd be touching the streets in a few hours and when he did it was going to be on. He was going to bring it to the cat that had set him up. And when he did that mothafucka was going to wish that he'd suffocated inside of his father's condom. After finishing the orange, Paybacc propped his feet upon the kid he'd hurt and folded his arms across his chest. He leant his head back against the wall and closed his eyes for a nap. He was going to need his shut eye if he was going to pump fear into the hearts of men.

TWENTY THREE

The day was a sweltering one. The heat was warming the streets. Folks took to wearing little to nothing to feel some sort of breeze while out and about. Some wore umbrella hats, while others wore wet towels over their heads and kept a bottle of water handy to fight off dehydration. The neighborhood kids took to water fights. Everything from water balloons to Super Soaker squirt guns were used in the water warfare. It being summer was the perfect excuse for the youngsters to wild out and have a good time.

Gouch and Banga emerged from out of the liquor store, each clad in tank tops and cargo shorts. They wore wet towels over their heads and their tank tops boasted sweat stains around the collar and backs.

"Yo, watch my back, I'm 'bout to roll up." Banga told Gouch as he went about the task of preparing a blunt for them to indulge in.

Gouch nodded and twisted the cap off of his Kiwi Strawberry Snapple, taking a long drink. He twisted the cap back on the Snapple while his eyes scanned the block for any approaching trouble.

"What chu got up for tonight, Nigga?" Banga asked, dumping the guts out of his Cigarillo.

"I'm 'pose to chill with this broad I bumped at the Slauson Slaughter House. Bitch proper, too." Gouch told him. "She gotta lil sista. You want me to see what's up?"

"How she look, Bro?"

"She's cute." Gouch assured him. "To tell you the truth I wish I would have got at lil sis, but I got up with old girl first."

"Well, shit, set it up then."

Gouch nodded and said, "I got chu."

Gouch pulled out his cell phone and placed a call to homegirl he'd bumped at the Slauson Swap Meet. A young African American man wearing an old Dodgers baseball cap and a beige and blue striped button-down with the sleeves rolled up made his way down the sidewalk. His hands gripped the handlebar of a pushcart with stickers advertising a variety of ice cream cones and bars on it. The gold bell that dangled from the handlebar of the pushcart rang as the man pushed the cart forth. The ringing bell was like a dog whistle for children how it drew the neighborhood kids in. Once he saw the kids enjoying their ice cream, Gouch decided that he wanted one.

"Hold on, Baby," Gouch said into the cell before turning to Banga. "Yo, you want something from off here?"

"Nah, I'm good." Banga sprinkled Kush throughout the blunt.

Gouch walked across the street to the pushcart chopping it up on his cell with homegirl. By the time he'd gotten there all of the kids had dispersed, leaving him and the young man alone. Gouch looked over the ice cream stickers on the pushcart trying to figure out what he wanted.

"Let me get a Napoleon sandwich bar." Gouch told the young man and went to reach inside of his pocket for the money.

The young man removed his baseball cap and wiped his sweaty forehead with a folded handkerchief. He then reached down inside of the square hole at the top of the pushcart.

"Man, I got one more left, it's all of the way up front but I can't reach it." The young man told him. "You mind?"

"All right, me and the homie gone slide through there 'bout nine. Peace." Gouch ended the call and slipped his cell back into the pocket of his cargo shorts. Gouch reached inside of the square hole and felt around for the Drumstick.

URRRRRRRRRRK!

A van came to a halt beside the pushcart and the door was thrown open by a masked man. On both sides of him were two masked men and they were gripping AK-47s. The masked man that had thrown open the van's door was mad dogging Gouch through the holes of his ski-mask. He clenched his teeth and hopped out of the van to snatch Gouch. Gouch went to draw his Girls from his waistline, but before he could the young man pulled out on him. Gouch slowly lifted his hands into the air, surrendering. The young man pressed his joint to the side of Gouch's dome and forced him inside of the van.

Gouch was roughly forced to the floor of the van and a black pillowcase was thrown over his head while his wrists were duct-taped behind his back. The young man tucked his joint into the small-of-his-back. He made to climb inside of the van when a slug slammed into the side of his dome. Blood, brain matter and pieces of skull went up into the air and came down like snowflakes on a cold winter night. The young man fell backwards into the street with his eyes bulged and his mouth stretched open.

The masked man threw the van's door closed just as Banga ran upon it with his smoking gun. Banga punched and pounded on the van's door. He started to pop a couple of holes through the door but the fear of accidentally killing Gouch stayed his hand. The van skirted off leaving Banga behind. Having not fully healed from his gunshot wounds, Banga was only able to skip along as he let his thang off behind the van.

BLOC! BLOC! BLOC! BLOC! BLOC! BLOC! BLOC!

Banga's banger jumped in his palm as he sent hot rocks at the rear of the van. Bullets slammed into the van's bumper, cracked its brake lights and shattered its left back window. Banga lost his balance and fell into the middle of the street. When he looked up the van was speeding away. Realizing that he'd failed to save his homeboy, Banga closed his eyes and let his forehead drop to the street.

$$$

Chingo sat behind the tattered oak wood desk taking casual pulls from a blunt as he thumbed through the hundreds of pictures of sexy naked women inside of his Samsung Galaxy. His lips parted and released white smoke. He inhaled deeply and drew the smoke back into his nostrils where he blew it back out in a cloud. He couldn't help but to reminisce about all of the tail he'd ran through in his day. He'd had the pleasure of slaying some of the most beautiful women you could imagine. The chicks he'd given the dick to was every rich niggaz lover and every poor niggaz dream. Ever since he'd hooked up with Yvette and they had Blessyn he'd put a stop to his whorish ways. He planned on settling down and given his baby boy a shot at a real family.

As Chingo continued to thumb through the pictures he came across some of Yvette, then some of them together and then finally one of she, him and Blessyn. Seeing them altogether warmed Chingo's heart. A smile stretched across his face, revealing his shiny gold grill. Chingo deleted all of the pictures of his jump offs, leaving only the ones of him and his family behind.

Hearing the shutter rising down stairs inside of the warehouse, Chingo slipped his cell phone into his pocket and got to his feet. He trekked across the office, walking upon the scattered papers on the floor until he reached the dirt smudged window that allowed you to see the entire warehouse. He watched as one of his henchmen pulled the chain and closed the shutter while the others rustled Gouch from out of the van.

The door of the office flew open and the henchmen came in with Gouch. One of the henchmen smacked an iron chair down at the center of the floor and planted Gouch in it. He then yanked the pillowcase from Gouch's head and took his place amongst the other henchmen. Chingo walked in Gouch's direction while taking pulls from his blunt. Gouch lifted his head slightly, glaring at Chingo and clenching his jaws tightly.

"What's up, Homie? I don't know if you remember me, but…" the words died in Chingo's throat when he saw Gouch wearing a knot on his forehead, a bloody nose and a busted lip. Chingo's brow furrowed as he looked at his henchmen, accusingly. "Fuck happened here?"

"Nigga was giving us trouble, so I had to sic these dogs on his ass." One of the henchmen spoke, lifting up his balled fists for emphasis.

"What part of safe and sound don't chu understand, Shaky?" Chingo frowned.

"Whatever, Man, we lost Dice tryna get this mothafucka."

Chingo's hand was like a blur when he drew steel and put two nickel sized holes in Shaky's face, dropping him where he stood.

The henchmen's mouths dropped open in shock. They looked down at Shaky's dead body and then over at Chingo. Chingo leveled his banger at Shaky's form and dumped two more shots into him. He then sat his weapon on the desk beside him.

"To hell with Dice," Chingo said looking over the masked faces of his henchmen. "That fool stayed fucking up, he couldn't get right for shit…Y'all give me and my man here a sec." With that said the henchmen filed out of the office, with the last of them pulling the door closed behind them.

Chingo blew out a roar of white smoke as he turned to his left and mashed out the blunt on the oak wood desk top. He tucked his banger on his waistline and approached Gouch, snatching up a chair along the way. He planted the chair before Gouch, twisting it around backwards, and sitting down.

"My bad, G, but good help is hard to find these days. Know what I'm saying?" Chingo waited for Gouch's response, but when he didn't get it he continued talking. "That day you caught me slipping in the parking lot at the Del Amo mall you could have let them toys sing me a lullaby but you didn't. You spared my skinny brown ass. You showed mercy where some of my homies probably wouldn't have. Had that had been Paybacc he would have banged me and my lil man and wouldn't have thought twice about it. For all of the stories I've heard about you being the offspring of Satan…I gotta tell you that day I didn't expect that."

"What did you bring me here for?" Gouch mad dogged him, his face twitching with anger.

"I brought you here because I figured that I'd have a better chance reasoning with you than that hot headed brother of yours." Chingo told him. "I'd like to propose a truce amongst our respective governing bodies. I'm not saying we've gotta be friends, I'm not even saying that we've gotta be cordial with one another. All I'm saying is let's stop this killing and get back to getting this money.

"I'm tired of burying my homies. I know you got to be tired of burying yours. Plenty of innocent people have been killed during this war. I know you've heard about that lil girl at that house party that caught a hold of some hot shit? That kid was five years old. Your brother gotta baby boy, right? Well, as you already know I gotta lil one also. And with these bullets flying every which way I'd hate to see something happen to either one of them, you know what I'm saying?" Gouch shot daggers in Chingo's direction for bringing up his nephew. Chingo raised his hands in surrender. "That's no underlined threat, Fam. I'm speaking on some real shit. Bullets ain't got no names."

For a time Gouch didn't say anything but Chingo could tell that he was letting the truce roll around inside of his head like a small metal ball inside of a pinball machine.

Gouch cleared his throat and looked up at Chingo.

"I can't call a truce on my word alone," Gouch admitted, "The word has to come down from baby bro. I have to link up with him and see how he wants to play this. I can't guarantee anything. I gotta see where his head is at."

Chingo nodded. He walked over to the office window, knocked and motioned for his henchmen to come back up. Moments later, the henchmen came filing through the door and surrounded Gouch. Chingo gave the one he called Cheese a nod. Cheese stepped before Gouch and unsheathed a Machete. The light in the ceiling bounced off of the shiny metal blade and made it glare. Gouch didn't even flinch when he saw him do this. He stared directly into Chingo's eyes without so much as batting an eye. Cheese slowly circled Gouch until he was standing directly behind him.

SNIKT!

With one swift motion of his Machete, Cheese freed Gouch from the duct-tape that bounded his wrists together. Gouch brought his arms around and ripped the rest of the duct-tape from his wrists. He looked up to see Chingo extending a slip of paper his way. He took the slip of paper and glanced over it. It was a telephone number.

"Holla at me once you get up with your brotha." Chingo told him. "I expect to hear from you in the next 48 hours…If not, the offer expires, and we're right back on that bullshit." He looked to Cheese. "Give the homie back his bangers when you drop him off."

Cheese nodded.

Chingo outstretched his hand in Gouch's direction. Gouch looked at Chingo's hand and then into his eyes. He allowed his hand to linger in the air for a time before finally shaking it.

"Let's go." Cheese told Gouch as he headed towards the door.

Gouch had just made it to the door when Chingo called after him.

"48 hours, my nigga."

Gouch nodded and continued through the door.

TWENTY FOUR

Gouch threw open the door of the van and jumped down into the street. Cheese ejected the magazines from the bottoms of his Berettas and handed them back to him. He then threw the door closed and the van drove off, calm and easy. Once the van was gone, Gouch jogged across the street to his car. Shit! He thought to himself seeing the parking ticket on his windshield. He snatched the ticket from under the windshield wiper and hopped into his ride. He resurrected the vehicle and pulled off, setting the navigation system for his first destination: Pavielle's house.

$$$

Pavielle, Killa Dre, Banga and a host of homies sat at the living room table loading and cocking submachine guns. All of the men were draped in black from head to toe and wearing Nike baseball gloves. A couple of Ls were in rotation amongst them. The living room was engulfed by so much weed smoke that you would have thought someone had left a fog machine running. Pavielle loaded his MP-5 and laid it upon the table. He picked up his glass of Cognac and brought it to his mouth. Seeing a flicker of movement at the corner of his eye, Pavielle froze the glass at his lips and looked to the doorway. Vayda stood there shooting daggers at him. The intensity her eyes emitted made him feel like he was about to burst into flames. He could practically feel the heat and see the vapors rising from her. The doorbell chimed. Vayda rolled her eyes and went to answer it.

"Bitch," Pavielle said under his breath and took a sip of the dark liquor. He looked to the front door and Vayda was unchaining and unlocking it. "Who is it?" he called out.

That's when Gouch came through the door. He hugged Vayda lovingly and pecked her on the cheek before heading into the living room where he saw everyone gathered. Pavielle sat his glass down and met his big brother halfway. The two gave each other a gangster's embrace.

"Fuck you been at, Blood? Me and the homies were 'bout to turn South Central into the Murder Capital." Pavielle balled up his face.

"On mommas, we were about to make the streets feel our pain." Killa Dre nodded as he gripped an AK-47.

"We thought you were dead, Bleed," Banga stated. He stood beside Killa Dre gripping a .45 in each of his gloved mitts.

"Y'all were 'bout to turn the city on its head behind my kidnapping, that's love for a homeboy for real." Gouch tapped his fist against his left breast, where his heart resided. "I'm straight though."

"Banga said that some niggaz snatched chu. What happened?" Pavielle asked seriously.

"I need to holla at chu, Bro." Gouch motioned for Pavielle to follow him into the other room. Pavielle grabbed his glass of Cognac and entered one of the bedrooms on the ground floor. Gouch closed the door behind him and turned around, lighting up a cigarette. He took a pull and expelled white smoke.

"It was Chingo's people that grabbed me up." Gouch told him. "He wants a truce."

"Mannnnn, I'm not even tryna..."

Gouch quickly interjected. "Let me finish. He said all he's tryna do is get his, and he can't do that with slugs flying back and forth from both sides. He says he wants it to go back how it was before: us getting money on our side and them getting money on theirs. I told him that we weren't seeing eye-to-eye with our plug right now and were looking for a new one. He told me that if we squash this shit that he'll connect us with his dude, and he was sure that he could negotiate a deal for fifteen a pie."

"Tell Chingo I said to take his truce and jam it up his mother's cunt." Pavielle said. Gouch closed his eyes, blew hard and brought his hands down his face. "The only way this thing ends is when he and Paybacc are lying on their backs with a pastor reciting their eulogies. I done lost too many people for me to let this shit ride 'cause these batty boys wanna throw in the towel. It's too late to go waving the white flag. I don't trust them dudes no way. For all you know this could be some kind of double cross."

"I feel what chu saying, I wasn't tryna hear homeboy out at first but he's willing to give us something to show that he's on the up and up. He's even willing to meet at a mutual spot to chop it up."

Pavielle was silent for a moment as he gave it some thought. He shook his head, "I don't know, Gucci."

"OK…Well, will you at least think on it?"

"Alright, you got that, but I'm not promising anything." Pavielle told him.

"Fair enough," Gucci said.

"I'm glad your back home." Pavielle embraced his big brother lovingly and kissed him on the cheek.

"I am, too." Gouch replied.

"Come on." Pavielle snatched open the door and made his exit.

Pavielle headed back inside of the kitchen and picked his glass of Cognac up from the counter. He brought the glass to his lips and was about to take a sip when he noticed the homies eyeballing him.

"Oh, y'all can take it home now. Big bro is Gucci." Pavielle told them. "I'll call y'all up once I figure out our next move."

The homies moved to the front door like a herd of cattle, Killa Dre and Gouch lagged behind chopping it up.

"What's popping, Outlaw?" Killa Dre asked.

"Chingo offered a truce, Man, but baby bro isn't sure if he's gonna take it."

"He's indecisive, huh?"

Gouch nodded and said, "We're supposed to visit our parents' graves tomorrow. I'm hoping he would have changed his mind by then."

"What if he doesn't budge?"

"Then we're still at war."

"Fuck it then." Killa Dre threw his hood over his black L.A snapback. "If we're still at odds with these faggots then so be it."

TWENTY FIVE

The next day

The school bell wailed loudly as the clock struck 2:30 P.M and brought the end to another day. For a time there was silence and then the doors of Western Avenue Elementary went flying open and children came pouring out of the hall and down the steps. While some of the children posted up in front of the school waiting for their parents to arrive, others hurriedly moved to board their buses or played the yard participating in after school activities.

JoJo and his friends kicked it underneath the shade of a tree talking about next to nothing as they played with their Yoyos. A familiar cadence of a nursery song ripped through the air and snagged all of the children's attention. Everyone looked up the block to see an ice cream truck approaching. The children's eyes lit up and they took off running towards the ice cream truck. When the ice cream truck pulled up in front of the school, the children swarmed it like a mass of angry bees, waving a fist of dollar bills.

One by one, a child broke off from the crowd of children at the ice cream truck, with his or her item of choice. JoJo was the last kid left. Once he'd gotten his ice cream the ice cream truck drove off down the street. A smile stretched across JoJo's face as he feasted his eyes on the Spider Man ice cream. He pulled off the wrapper and revealed a bust of Spider Man with pink bubble gum eyes. JoJo threw the wrapper aside and headed off to rejoin his quartet of friends.

Hearing a horn being honked, JoJo looked over his shoulder and saw his mother's Scion down the street. An arm extended out of the window and waved him over. JoJo waved goodbye to his friends and headed towards his mother's car, indulging in his Spider Man ice cream. JoJo got about ten feet from his mother's Scion before he noticed that it wasn't her behind the wheel. What he saw was a man with a thick nappy beard and big lens glasses. He wore a colorful Rastafarian beanie over his thick dread locks. His body bulged with muscles and was covered by a fishnet tank top.

"What's up, Young JoJo?" the Rasta said in a heavy Jamaican accent.

"I don't talk to strangers."

"I'm not a stranger, me know your father, Boy." The Rasta told him. "Me a friend of his; we grew up together."

"How come I never seen you at my house then?" he looked at him side ways.

"Me went back to me homeland, I came back out here to visit your old man." the Rasta said. "Your mudda is entertaining company at ya house so she asked me to pick ya up." JoJo shot the Rasta a look like 'Nigga, your lying'. "You don't believe me, huh? I'll show you a picture of me and ya parents. Come here."

The Rasta lifted his ass off of the seat and pulled what JoJo guessed was his wallet from out of his back pocket. JoJo looked both ways before jogging across the street to his mother's Scion. When he reached the driver side door he saw the Rasta wetting a rag with chloroform. JoJo moved to run but the Rasta snatched him inside through the window, causing him to drop his Spider Man ice cream in the street. JoJo kicked and thrashed around. He screamed and the Rasta pressed the rag over the lower half of his face. JoJo's movements slowed until he became still. He lay in the Rasta's arms looking through narrowed eyed with an open mouth. He was unconscious.

Paybacc looked around to make sure no one was looking before he slid JoJo into the passenger seat and buckled him in. He then resurrected the Scion and pulled away from the scene, cranking the volume up on the stereo.

$$$

"Creg, did Andrea make it back from picking up JoJo yet?"

"Nuh uh, Miss Gavens, she hasn't made it back home yet." Cheese said, cradling the phone to his ear with his shoulder and licking a blunt closed. "She's supposed to be stopping at the nail salon first though. She should be back…" he looked at the time on the Time Warner cable box. It was 4:30 P.M. "She should be back any minute now. I'll have her call you as soon as she gets back."

"When was the last time you spoke to her?"

"Around two o'clock."

"Creg, I think something is wrong. I've called her a couple of times today and she hasn't answered."

"Miss Gavens, you're jumping to conclusions, I'm sure everything is OK." Cheese assured her. "She probably forgot to cut the ringer back on her cell phone. She puts it on vibrate when she's at work."

"Creg, call me paranoid if you want, but I know something isn't right." Miss Gavens told him. "Something is up, I can just feel it."

"I'll tell you what, Mother in Law; let's give her thirty more minutes." Cheese told her. "If she hasn't come home by then, I'll bend a couple of corners and see what's up, how's that?"

"No," Miss Gavens quickly responded. "In thirty minutes I want you to come pick me up so I can file a missing persons report down at the police station."

"If it will make you feel better, I'm all for it."

"OK then, Creg, I'll see you in thirty minutes."

"You got it."

They hung up.

Cheese lay back on his black leather sofa, taking pulls from his blunt and blowing white smoke rings into the air. He took a few more tokes of the blunt and turned on the flat-screen. An episode of the old HBO series OZ popped on the screen. He watched the show while he took casual drags from the blunt. Before long his eyes had narrowed into slits and were red and glassy. He licked his dry lips and felt a thirst for alcohol invade his brain. He rose to his feet and mobbed inside of the kitchen. He grabbed a glass from out of the cupboard, dropped a couple of ice cubes inside of it and snatched a bottle of Hennessy from off the top of the refrigerator, along with a red can of Coca Cola. Next, he poured a little of the Coke into the glass and twisted off the cap of the Hennessy bottle. He went to pour some into the glass when he felt his cell phone vibrate in his pocket. That's when he decided to sit the Hennessy bottle down on the counter and pulled out his cell phone. A smile spread across his face when he saw Draya on the screen. Paranoid, he shook his head as he thought of how

Miss Gavens had been acting. He then pressed answer on his cell phone and brought it to his ear.

"What's up, Baby?" he spoke into the cell phone as he poured up the Hennessy.

"What's up is, you bringing your punk ass up here 'fore I off wifey and this punk ass son of yours. God knows I'd be doing the world a favor by ridding it of another bitch ass nigga."

Cheese's face twisted into something hideous, giving him the appearance of some sort of monster. He was furious and it registered on his face.

"Cuz, who the fuck is this?"

"Baby," Cheese's wife, Draya, came on the phone sobbing, "this man has me and JoJo here and he says he's going to kill us if you don't come where we are!"

"Come where?" Cheese asked, finally realizing this whole ordeal wasn't a game and should be taken very seriously. "Where are y'all?"

"Listen closely, 'cause I'm not going to repeat myself…" Paybacc came back on the phone. He gave Cheese the address to his location and he hastily wrote it down on his palm with a black Sharpie marker.

"I swear 'fore God, Nigga, if you do anything to hurt mines, I'ma…" that was as far as Cheese got before Draya's screams drowned him out.

"That was wifey's ring finger," Paybacc told him. Hearing Paybacc say that coupled with Draya's screams caused Cheese to drop to his knees. Tears welled up in his eyes and spilled down his cheeks. He wiped them away as quickly as they came, but they just kept on coming. "Now you threaten me again and I'll chop off her whole mothafucking hand, comprende, Ese? Do we understand each other?" By this time Cheese was leaning against the island in the kitchen with the cell phone pressed to his ear. He fought back the tears and tried to pull himself together. He didn't want to speak until he was sure his voice was void of emotion. It was important to him to remain a gangster under the circumstances.

"Yeah, I got chu, I got chu." Cheese nodded, cradling the cell phone to his ear.

"Alright then. You've got an hour to get here." Paybacc made it clear. "I'm cutting off a finger every minute after that so I suggest you put a move on it."

As soon as Paybacc hung up, Cheese tucked his banger on his waistline and grabbed his jacket on the way out of the door, so much for Miss Gavens' paranoia.

$$$

Paybacc stood over a gagged and bound JoJo and Draya admiring the platinum and diamond engagement ring on her severed finger.

"This mothafucka chunky, Cuz," Paybacc said of the ring. "What's this, fourteen karats? Princess cut, pink and yellow stones? Whew, these mothafuckaz aren't cloudy either." He looked to the tear streaked face of Draya. "Lil' Momma, you must be sitting on some wet, wet for Cheese's bitch ass to come off the paper for this rock. Welp, it's mine now." Using his teeth, he pulled the diamond ring off of the severed finger and slipped it into his pocket. He then chucked the severed finger aside and approached a whimpering JoJo.

He stuck his Desert Eagle under the boy's chin and tilted his head up so that he'd be looking directly into his eyes. JoJo's face was slick wet and he was shaking uncontrollably.

"Don't fret, Lil' Cuz, yo punk ass daddy will be here in a minute and then this will be all over with." Paybacc leant up against the side of the van, whistling as he searched his cell phone for a video game to play.

TWENTY SIX

Cicero and Maddy stood before Pavielle inside of the living room. He'd just chambered a live round into his .9mm and tucked it into the small of his back. He was now slipping on a wave-cap and sports coat.

Gouch was coming to scoop Pavielle up so that they could ride out to Inglewood Cemetery to visit the grave sites of their Loved Ones. Every Friday, since they were kids G-momma would take them to buy fresh Dandelions from the flower shop to place on their parents' graves. As adults the Hood Brothers continued with this tradition. Unfortunately, they'd lost more Loved Ones over the course of time and had to purchase significantly more flowers.

"Under no circumstances is she to leave this house with my son. If she wants to bounce on her own accord then let her go." Pavielle told them. "Do we understand one another?" his eyes shifted from Cicero to Maddy. They nodded. "Good."

The entire time Pavielle was giving Cicero and Maddy instructions; Vayda was glaring at him from where she sat on the couch, breast feeding their son. Pavielle kissed his offspring on the forehead and headed for the front door. Once Pavielle was gone, Cicero and Maddy plopped down on the love seat. Cicero picked up the remote control and turned on the flat-screen; while Maddy didn't waste any time preparing herself a blunt.

"See if Sons of Anarchy is on," Maddy told Cicero. "I missed it this Tuesday."

"All right," Cicero flipped through the channel and lucked up on the episode of Sons of Anarchy that they'd missed.

"Yeah, this is my shit."

"Where are my manners?" Vayda said to no one in particular. "How would you guys like some fried chicken and rice?"

"Hell yeah, hook that up." Maddy said.

"I haven't eaten all day, good looking out, Sis." Cicero added.

"Just let me lay lil man down and I can rustle that up."

Once Vayda had left, Maddy tapped Cicero.

"Yo, you don't think it's kind of weird that homegirl's being all hospitable and shit, after she laid the smack down on you that time?"

Cicero shrugged.

"Bitch probably bored. Booby keeps her cooped up in here all of the time. I mean, she's gotta find something to do with herself, right?"

"I guess." Maddy said, licking the blunt closed.

$$$

"Have you at least thought about the proposition Chingo presented us with?" Gouch glanced over at Pavielle. They were standing over the headstones of their parents. Pavielle had just sat a bouquet of flowers on each of their graves and kissed the headstones.

"Yeah, I thought about it." Pavielle admitted. "I figure these fools are only looking for a truce 'cause they know the heat is on and their chicken shit asses are about to be fried extra crispy, ya dig me? We've got 'em right where we want them Gucci, they're scared now. You can't see that? It's not about the money they're just tryna save face."

"Still," Gouch began, "Wouldn't this be a great opportunity to take advantage of? He's giving us a supplier and he's willing to call off his dogs. We could get back to making this money without having to worry about catching a hot one. The way I see it, it's a win, win situation for us. Let's capitalize off of it."

Pavielle blew hard as he thought about it.

"All right, let's make it happen." Pavielle finally agreed, causing Gouch to grin. "But I want the plug and one other thing. If he refuses me this other thing then he can go fuck himself. You got it?"

"I got chu." Gouch nodded. "Are you gone let me make this call to set up this meeting?" he looked hopeful.

"Go ahead." Pavielle told him.

Smiling, Gouch pulled out his cell phone and punched in some numbers.

"Yo, Chingo, I spoke to my brother, Man. He wants to connect." Gouch spoke into his cell. "Where you tryna meet up?"

$$$

Vayda stood inside of the living room with her arms folded across her chest. Her eyes looked from Cicero to

Maddy. They were both fast asleep having devoured their food and drunk the ice tea she'd tainted with sleeping pills.

Vayda moved like the wind blew, getting dressed and gathering a couple of things for the baby. Once she was done, she took a Christian Louboutin shoe box full of cash from the walk-in closet and dumped its contents into the baby's diaper bag. She then retrieved her sleek black .22 with the ivory handle from the bottom dresser drawer. After checking its magazine and cocking it, she dropped it into her clutch. She scooped up the baby seat, which Little Nasheed was in, and headed for the door.

$$$

"The meeting goes down tomorrow at one o'clock." Gouch informed Pavielle after ending his conversation with Chingo.

"Where?" Pavielle asked.

"Ross Snyder's park."

"Cool." Pavielle nodded. "I want a couple of gunners there an hour before in case homeboy is living foul. At the first sign of trouble I want his skull capped like a New York nigga, ya Griff me?"

"All day," Gouch replied.

$$$

Mark and Bleezy sat parked a block away from Pavielle's mansion. They had been watching the place for the past hour waiting for him to make an appearance so they could send him somewhere real hot. They had a serious hard-on for the young kingpin, but Vayda or the baby would also do. Their quota was 50 grand a head, with promises of an extra 25 if they brought back the kingpin's severed head. Their employer wanted to get it bronzed and hang it over his fireplace like a deer's head.

"We've got movement." Bleezy announced as he peered through the windshield. He quickly capped the Hennessy bottle and sat it between his legs. Mark resurrected the Honda station wagon and pulled off. He tailed the black Mercedes that had just rolled out of the gates of the mansion.

$$$

Vayda sang along to R. Kelly's "You Saved Me" as it pulsated through the speakers. She tickled her baby boy's chin causing him to giggle and flail his little arms. She looked from the windshield to Little Nasheed as she sang to him. His being born had done just that, saved her life. With his birth she felt like she was re-born and had gotten a second chance at life, a chance to start over and become a better person than she was before.

Vayda glanced up at the rearview mirror and saw an Explorer Sport hastily approaching. She started not to pay it any mind but something told her that she should be concerned. With that in mind, she continued to sing as she let her hand dip inside of her clutch and withdraw the .22. She rested the hand gripping the pistol in her lap and kept an eye on the Explored through the rearview mirror.

$$$

"Grab them thangs out the back," Mark told Bleezy as they were coming upon the Mercedes. When Bleezy turned around to grab the weapons from off the backseat, through the back window he saw a car speeding towards them. Bleezy grabbed two KG-9s. He kept one for himself and passed the other to Mark.

"We've got a car coming up." Bleezy informed his partner-in-crime. "You wanna fall back until it passes us up?"

Mark glanced at the rearview mirror and saw the car coming up from the rear.

"Fuck 'em!" Mark answered. "We'll rock the ski-masks and if this mothafucka sticks his nose into our business he's road kill."

Mark and Bleezy pulled their ski-masks down over their faces.

Bleezy held down a switch and the front passenger window descended.

$$$

Pavielle's cell phone rang. He glanced at the screen and then answered it.

"What's popping?" he spoke into his cell. The news he got caused his face to contort with anger. "The fuck you mean she's gone? How the hell did she get away when y'all supposed to be watching her? Shit!" he pounded the dashboard with his fist.

"What happened?" Gouch asked.

"Vayda left with my seed." Pavielle told him. "We've gotta hurry up and get home, Man."

Pavielle focused his attention back on the caller.

"Y'all stay put; we're on our way back."

As soon as Pavielle ended the call, his cell rang and vibrated in his palm.

He showed Gouch who it was and they exchanged knowing glances.

$$$

Vayda unbuckled the safety belt and got a firm grip on the .22. She glanced into the side view mirror and saw the Explorer gaining up on her. Her palms dampened from sweat and her heart beat like an African drum against the interior of her chest. She said a quick silent prayer and took a couple deep breaths. She hoped that she was just paranoid but that hope was banned from her mental when she saw a masked gunman emerge from the Explorer's front passenger window gripping a KG-9. Oh shit! She thought aloud, her eyes bulging and mouth opening. Shit had just gotten real.

Pat! Pat! Pat! Pat!

The driver side window imploded and peppered Vayda with glass. She looked to her son and he was wailing. All she could think about was his and her survival. The thought of someone snatching the most precision thing in her life from her was devastating. Her face projected the hurt and anger she felt. Her maternal instincts kicked into overdrive and she clenched her teeth. Madness danced in her eyes and she growled. Clutching her .22, she pointed it out of the window just as the masked gunman came into her line of vision.

Pow! Pow!

The masked gunman howled in pain and squeezed the trigger of his KG-9 as it fell in a spiral, blowing holes in the side of the Benz and bursting its front tire. Vayda gripped the steering wheel and slammed on the brakes. The sudden stop propelled the Benz forward and sent it tumbling ahead. The Benz landed on its roof and skidded down the street.

Vayda lie on the ceiling of the Benz covered in broken glass. Her face was bloody and littered with tiny cuts. Hearing the wailing of her baby boy, she slowly began to stir awake. Her eyes fluttered open and she looked to the front passenger seat. Little Nasheed was suspended upside down in the baby seat, held in place by the safety belt. Vayda moved to release him when something latched onto her crown of sandy brown curls.

"Ahhhhh," Vayda screamed as the masked gunman began to drag her from out of the wrecked Benz. She tried grabbing a hold of something as she was being drug but ended up slicing up her hands on the broken glass. Vayda bit down on her bottom lip as fire engulfed both of her hands. A twinkle at the corner of her eye got her attention. She looked and found a long shard of glass. Swiftly, she snatched the shard and drove it into the masked gunman's sneaker. The masked gunman let go of a blood curdling scream but kept his hold on Vayda.

"Fucking cunt," he pulled Vayda out into the street and threw her up against the side of the Benz. He snatched the glass shard out of his foot and stood erect. His partner came to stand beside him. They pointed their KG-9s at Vayda and rested their fingers against the triggers. Vayda swallowed hard and squeezed her eyes closed, praying for a quick death.

Boc! Boc! Boc! Bo! Boc!

Boc! Boc! Boc! Boc! Boc!

The gunfire ceased.

Vayda's heart pounded in her ears. She inhaled the fumes of gun smoke and fresh blood. Her eyes peeled opened and she looked around. A cherry red Hummer was idling in the middle of the street. Pavielle was hanging out of the front passenger window gripping his .9mm with both hands. Gouch was standing up in the sunroof clutching both of his Girls. A grin emerged on Vayda's face, she'd never been so happy to see her fiancé in all of the time they'd been together.

Vayda crawled back inside of the wrecked Benz and released Little Nasheed from the safety belt. When she rose to her feet with the baby in her arms see saw Pavielle on his cell phone. He'd just opened the door and stepped out into the street when she rushed over and hugged him.

"How did you know that they would be after her?" Pavielle asked the caller.

"Because I sent them."

"What?" Pavielle frowned.

"You heard me." Black Jesus told him. "I had to send you a message."

"And that is?" Pavielle frowned.

"That you can be touched," Black Jesus answered. "Let this be a lesson, My Friend, 'cause should you ever disrespect me again I will destroy everything you hold dear."

Black Jesus disconnected the call.

Pavielle looked at his cell phone as if it were covered in slime. He then embraced Vayda lovingly and kissed his son on top of the head.

TWENTY SEVEN

That night

Pavielle stood outside the emergency entrance of UCLA hospital on the side of the Hummer. At the rear of the beast there were four black on black Mercedes Benz G wagons loaded with homies willing to kill and die on the young kingpin's orders. Gouch had made the arrangements for Pavielle to move like this where ever he went. He wanted his baby brother to be guarded at all times. If Pavielle went to take a piss Gouch wanted two men inside of the rest room with him and two more waiting outside of the rest room for him. From now on Pavielle was going to be moving around like he was the president of the United States with his own ensemble of Secret Service Agents.

Pavielle stared down at the screen saver of his family as he waited for Vayda to be discharged from the hospital. His thumb caressed the display of his cell phone and the smirk that inhabited his face blossomed into a full blown smile. At that moment, staring at the screen, he couldn't help but feel like the luckiest son of a bitch on earth. His family was like his good luck charm. As long as he had them he thought that there wasn't anything he couldn't get through. Having them in his heart made him feel like he was invincible. Like there wasn't any obstacle he couldn't overcome or any challenge that couldn't be met. His Loved Ones gave him the genuine feeling that he could take on the world all by himself and come out victorious. It was then that he realized that though his family was his strength they were also his weakness. And if anything should ever happen to them he'd crumble like a stale cookie. He didn't even want to fathom the heart ache that their deaths would bring him. The thought alone would leave him as competent as a vegetable mentally. This was why he was going to go through with the plan he'd formulated earlier.

Pavielle had just slipped his cell phone into his pocket when Vayda emerged through the double doors of the emergency entrance. The tiny cuts on her face had been cleaned up and her hands had been wrapped in bandages. Her makeup had run from crying, her hair was a mess and her clothes looked like they'd seen better days. Vayda looked like she'd been raped, stabbed, shot and drug through hell twice. She felt like it too.

Pavielle motioned Vayda over as he held open the front passenger door. She ducked inside and he closed the door shut behind her. He then whipped out his .9mm and hurried around to the other side. He hopped inside and slammed the door shut behind him. Seeing the joint in his hand made Vayda uneasy. Her heart quickened and she scooted against the door.

"Easy," Pavielle chuckled and looked to the banger in his palm. "I got this out 'cause I don't want it digging into my hip."

He tucked the banger in between the seat and console. He resurrected the Hummer and pulled off with the G wagons trailing him.

"Where's the baby?" she looked to the backseat.

"He's back at the house with his uncle and God Father and about fifteen of the homies." Pavielle told her. "Don't worry he's all right. Won't shit happen to him that won't happen to them first."

"You gotta square?" she asked.

Pavielle nodded and said, "Ashtray."

Vayda grabbed the carton of Newport 100s and withdrew a Joe. She slipped it between her lips and fired it up. Pulling the smoke into her lungs she felt a since of calm wash over her. Her nerves were jacked and the nicotine was just what the doctor ordered.

"You, all right?"

"Yeah," She nodded and tossed the Bic lighter into the ashtray.

"V, grab those bags outta the glove-box for me, will ya?"

Vayda opened the glove -box and pulled out two Zip-loc freezer bags of crisp stacks of Benjamin Franklins. The bags were crammed with so many bills that they were starting to split at their seams. Vayda sat the bags in her lap and looked to Pavielle wearing a mask of confusion.

"What's this for?"

Pavielle ignored her and continued, "Look in the sun-visor and take down the passports and the airline tickets."

Vayda did as she was instructed.

"Miami?" Vayda asked after reading over one of the airline tickets.

"Yes, I want you and the baby far from here. It's the only way I can be sure that you're all right." Pavielle told her. "Shit may get real nasty down here and I want you and the baby out of harm's way."

"Pavy, I don't..." Her emotions choked back her words. She felt stinging and warmth in her eyes as they began to mist. Tears trickled down her rose gold cheeks and she wiped her eyes with her finger. "Are you going to be all right?"

"I don't know." He said honestly.

Seeing her crying, he grabbed a couple of tissues from out of the glove-box and passed them to her. He watched her dab away her tears. That was all of the confirmation he needed to know that she was still in love with him.

"Don't wet it." Pavielle said. "Look at it this way. You'll finally be able to take Lil' Man and get away like you wanted. And this time I'm sponsoring it."

"That's not what I wanted." She shook her head and dried her eyes with the tissues. "I wanted you. I wanted for all of us to be a family. But with this beef and Gangsta, and G-momma being killed you turned into someone different. You turned into someone I didn't recognize anymore. You transformed into this monster driven by power and vengeance. At night, when you would sleep, I'd look at chu and couldn't help but to wonder who you were. It was like a stranger was lying in bed beside me."

"I know. I fucked up, Boo, I lost it." He took his hand from the steering wheel and grasped hers affectionately. "I'm your fiancé and the father of our child. I'm supposed to love, provide, and protect you. You're supposed to feel safe whilst in my presence. Not walking on pins and needles and afraid to say anything to me 'cause you fear it may set me off. That's not how it's supposed to be, Babe. I wanna get back to that space we were in when we first met. I want to be the husband and father you and Nasheed need me to be, ya Griff me?"

Vayda nodded yes.

"Everything is going to be all right, OK?"

"OK."

"I need you to say that you believe me." Pavielle told her. "Look me in the eyes and tell me that you believe me."

Vayda stared into his eyes and told him, "I believe you."

Pavielle smirked and kissed Vayda's fingers. He then brought her hand down beside him, caressing it with his thumb.

$$$

Pavielle and Vayda stood in the middle of the LAX, surrounded by people going to catch a flight or coming from off one. Though they were in the company of others the only people they were focused on were each other and their new born son. Pavielle had him cradled in his arms and was saying his final goodbye to him. It was a sentimental moment and Vayda couldn't stop the tears from falling. They seemed to flow like they were coming from a faucet and the tissues she had did little to combat them.

"…So you take care of mom for me all right, Son? I love you." Pavielle kissed his baby boy on the cheek and then his forehead. He held his head against his offspring for a time and then passed him to his mother.

Vayda placed the baby back into the baby seat and made sure that he was secure before covering him with a blanket. She then turned to her lover. They stared into one another's eyes having so much to say but not knowing where to begin. Then it happened, Vayda hugged and embraced him as tight as she could. She closed her eyes and took a deep breath. She could spend an eternity trapped in this moment with him. If it was up to her she'd never let him go. They'd fly out to Miami together and leave all of the drama behind in Cali. As badly as she wanted to suggest it she knew that Pavielle wouldn't go for it. He'd look at it as tucking his tail and running. He was a lot of things but he wasn't a coward. And he wasn't about to give anyone a reason to even think it.

Looking over Vayda's shoulder Pavielle saw people entering the line to board the flight to Miami. He broke his embrace with Vayda and held her at arm's length.

"You better get going, or you'll miss your flight."

"OK." she cupped his face with her hands and stared into his eyes. Tears slid down her cheeks and he swept them away with his thumbs. They then kissed long and passionately. Pavielle placed one last kiss on her forehead and walked away. He got about six feet before she called after him. He turned right around.

"I didn't mean what I said at home back in the theater." She confessed. "I've always loved you. I always will. My love for you flows like a fountain, it keeps growing and growing every day and I don't know how to turn it off."

Pavielle nodded. He watched her turn around and head to the line for her flight.

Pavielle strode out of the double doors of the terminal and hopped into the front passenger seat of the Hummer. He picked up the half smoked L from the ashtray and lit it up. He blew out a cloud of white smoke and fanned it away from his face.

"Where we at with it?" Gouch asked.

"Ross Snyder's park," Pavielle answered.

TWENTY EIGHT

Cheese drove into the old warehouse. The headlights of his truck illuminated Draya and his eight year old son, JoJo. They were on their knees with their wrists bound behind their backs wearing gags and blindfolds. A hulk of a man stood behind them wearing a blue bandana on the lower half of his face and black sunglasses over his eyes. His leather gloved hand was wrapped around the handle of a Desert Eagle. Cheese could feel the tension coming off of him, which let him know that he wasn't for any bullshit.

Cheese stopped the Suburban a couple of feet from where Paybacc and his family were. He threw open the driver side door and hopped out onto the graveled ground. He made his way around the Suburban and posted up at its grill. Clutched in his hand was a Taurus .9mm. Paybacc made a quick mental note of the weapon but didn't order him to disgard it. The way he saw it he was in control of the situation and Cheese would do exactly what he was told. He knew he wouldn't do anything that would jeopardize the well being of his family.

"Here I am, just like you ordered." Cheese told Paybacc. "Now, let my family go so you and I can play with these thangs." He referred to them getting active with the guns until one of them was laid out leaking.

"Bitch, I'm calling the shots here, and ain't nobody leaving until I tell 'em to"

"You got it my nigga, this yo show."

"You mothafucking right it is, and don't chu forget it." Paybacc pointed his Desert Eagle in Cheese's direction and used his free hand to douse Draya and JoJo with a red gas-can full of gasoline. Once he'd finished with the red gas-can he set it aside.

"Chill, Homeboy!" Cheese held up his hands.

"Fuck a chill, I'm hot, Homes!" Paybacc barked heatedly. "Now I know it was you that planted that coke inside of my car, but what I wanna know is why?"

"Chingo wanted peace between the slobs, so that the streets could cool down and we could push this new product he got on deck." Cheese told him.

"And he knew that I wasn't going for that bygone shit, so he had you put that work in my car and call The Ones on me. Am I right?" Paybac asked having figured it all out.

Cheese nodded.

"You and Chingo are some snake ass bitches, you know that?" Payback barked. "You betrayed your brother behind greed. That's some weak ass shit."

"It wasn't all about the money, we got sick of seeing the homies die."

"Fuck outta here, is that what Chingo told you?" Paybacc asked, but didn't wait for him to answer. "I've known cuz since he was a pup, money is his motivator. Everything else is secondary."

"All right, Cuz, you got me balls here, so now, what?"

"Now what you ask? Now you get to watch your family die." Paybacc said with meancing eyes. "Say sayonara to the wife and kid, Baby Boy." His thumb struck the round metal ball of a Zippo lighter in a downward motion and a reddish orange flame came into existence.

Cheese got down on his knees and sat his banger beside him. He put his hands together about to plead for the lives of his family. "Paybacc, I'm begging you, Cuz, don't do this! Besides the set, my wife and my son are all I have." Tears formed in his eyes and his bottom lip quivered making him look like a sad ass puppy dog. "I'm sorry, my nigga, if I could reverse the decision I made, I would."

Cheese could tell that Paybacc was smiling beneath the blue bandana. The hardcore gangster got a kick out of watching his enemy grovel on his knees. Cheese didn't care though. He'd humiliate himself even further if it meant the lives of his Loved Ones would be spared. Paybacc held the Zippo lighter above JoJo's head, allowing it to dangle while its flame danced in the air. Cheese's eyes bulged and his mouth dropped open when Paybacc released the Zippo lighter from the pinch of his finger and thumb. While the Zippo lighter was in freefall, Cheese snatched up his banger and pointed it at Paybacc.

Blam! Blam! Blam! Blam! Blam! Blam! Blam!

Sweltering bullets lit Cheese's ass up, entering his front and exiting out of his back. His blood dashed the ground as he spun around like a ballerina and hit the surface. He lay twisted with red streams rolling from underneath his body. His eyes were bulging and his mouth was wide open. He took his last breath and went still. The Zippo lighter hit the ground and snapped closed. Paybacc lowered his Desert Eagle to his side. Even through their gags he could hear Draya and JoJo sob over the loss of Cheese. Paybacc picked up the red gas-can and guzzled the last of its contents thirstily. The water left him feeling replenished.

After slinging the empty red gas-can aside, Paybacc took a box cutter and cut Draya and JoJo loose. He watched as they rushed over to Cheese, crying and trying desperately to shake him awake. Paybacc jumped into the van, resurrected the engine and drove out of the warehouse.

With Cheese old buster ass taking an eternal nap, Paybacc moved to knock Chingo out of the box. He'd concocted a plan while he was leaning on Cheese's family that would leave him as the last man standing. With this devious plan he wouldn't even have to go looking for Chingo, he'd come to him on his own accord. Paybacc had the trap, but he needed someplace to spring it. He had just the place in mind and with a little incentive he was sure the tenant would go along with what he had planned.

"Ayo, Ed, let me holla at chu for a second!" Paybacc called out to Fast Talking Eddie with a hand cupped beside his mouth. At the moment Eddie was panhandling, trying come up on a few dollars for a couple of rocks. When he heard Payabcc calling for him he glanced over his shoulder. He narrowed his eyes and peered closely trying to see who it was asking for him. Thinking it was someone he had wronged in the past while on a mission to gather some scratch for his habit, he started to take off in the opposite direction but hearing the person say that they were 'Paybacc' made him relax and sigh with relief.

"Boss Hog, is that really you, Folks?" Eddie cautiously approached, holding hand above his brow so that he could see if it was really the O.G that called upon him.

"Yeah, it's me, Cuz."

"Aww, Man, I thought the Fuzz was gone have you for a long stay." Eddie told him. "You just gave dem crackas a visit, huh?" he slapped hands with Paybacc.

"I'm out on bail, Homie."

"Oh, that's what it is then."

"You still squatting in that crib around the way?"

"Yessir, what, you need some place to crash?"

"Nah, nothing like that, I need to borrow it though."

"Oh yeah, for what?"

"Never mind that, I gotta G-Ball with your name on it." Paybacc told him. "But when I'm done with that mothafucka you can't return. Ya hear me?"

"Man, fuck that house, I could always find a new spot to lay my head." Eddie said. "You won't it? It's yours, now, about that paper." He licked his chops and rubbed his hands together greedily.

"It's close by." Paybacc informed him. "Hop in the car."

"Alright."

Eddie damn near broke his neck dash around the car and hopping into the front passenger seat.

Paybacc was surprised when he crossed the threshold into Eddie's pad. The four bedroom house was tidy and furnished. Payabcc had been expecting the grand father of all shitholes before he walked into the place. He was convinced that he was going to see a house unfit to live in, but he was wrong. Eddie's crib was well kept by anyone's standards. Paybacc had to admit that he was impressed.

Paybacc nodded his head as he took in the full scope of the living room. He then turned around to Eddie, tossing him a bankroll secoured by a beige rubber-band. Eddie tucked the bankroll into his pocket and had made to leave when Paybacc called him back.

"Don't ever come back here, Man."

"You done beat it in my head a thousand times, Boss Hog. I got chu." Eddie told him. "I gotta breeze, Folks."

Paybacc watched Eddie run out of the house and into the night. There wasn't any doubt in his mind that he was going to make some Dope Boy a thousand dollars richer. Paybacc closed the closed the front door and headed into the kitchen. He sat the greasy brown paper bag on the table and sat his slice of cheese cake inside of the refrigerator. Removing his cell phone from his pocket, he sat down, and propped his sneakers upon the kitchen table. Paybacc placed a call to Chingo and brought the cell phone to his ear. Listening to the line ring, he examined his dirty finger nails. The line rang twice before Chingo picked up.

"What's crack-a-lacking?"

"It's on now, Cuz, niggaz tried to twist my shit back."

"For real?"

"Hell yeah, just now," Paybacc told him. "I had to get low at this smoker fool house."

"Where at?"

"I'ma give you the address, you gotta pen?"

"Hold on."

An evil smile spread across Paybacc's face as he waited for Chingo to find a pen to write the address down. He was giddy inside. He couldn't believe how easy this was going to be for him. Once Chingo came back on the cell phone Paybacc gave him the address and disconnected the call. He checked the magazine of his Desert Eagle and smacked it back into the bottom of his weapon. He then went about the task of eating his food while he waited for Chingo's arrival. As soon as he stepped foot inside of the house he was going to open up the front of his face.

TWENTY NINE

Ross Snyder's park was dark save for the dim lights illuminating over the basketball court. They shined upon the men that had gathered there for underworld dealings.

"You're late." Chingo told Pavielle once he'd approached.

"My fault, you know how this L.A traffic is. You're a native." Pavielle offered a weak excuse. Truth be told, he didn't give a fuck about being late. If Chingo and his buddy didn't like it they could kiss his skinny black ass.

"Whatever, Fam," Chingo turned to the tall, lanky cat standing beside him and tapped his arm. "This is my man, Sazoo; he's the dude I was telling you about that could help you with what we talked about."

"Right," Pavielle examined the tall, pale yellow cat in the linen short sleeve shirt and shorts. His head was bald all of the way around while the top of his crown was twisted in small locks. A beaded necklace hung from his neck and at the end of it was a large fist. His ears were weighed down by wood earrings with sapphires in them.

"Pleasure," Sazoo cracked a slight grin and extended his mitt to Pavielle.

Pavielle allowed Sazoo's hand to linger before shaking it, giving him a nod.

"Soooo, you wanted fifteen a kilo, right?" Sazoo spoke. "You purchase fifty birds from me at a time and I'll let chu get 'em for that price, deal?"

"Deal." He shook Sazoo's hand. He then looked to Chingo, "As for our business."

"I'll leave you two gentlemen be." Sazoo said, turning to Chingo. "You owe me one, Big Brudda."

"No doubt," Chingo replied.

Once Sazoo had climbed into his Cadillac Escalade and drove out of the park, Pavielle addressed Chingo about the rest of their business.

"In order for me to set forth in motion this truce between my people and yours I'm going to need one more thing from you, Pimp."

Chingo blew hard and folded his arms across his chest.

"What is it?"

Pavielle told Chingo what he needed in order to call a truce between them. He watched Chingo closely as he massaged his chin and thought about it. Pavielle secretly hoped he declined his request so that he could give the signal to his young boys to cut his ass down. None the less, he was quite surprised by the reply he received.

"Alright," Chingo nodded. "But this sit-down between us never happened, 'cause should it ever come to light my people would have my head."

"You have my word."

Pavielle stuck his pinky fingers into the sides of his mouth and whistled. A moment later, two masked up goons came running from out of the shadows with AK-47s. Chingo was surprised when he saw them. He didn't have a clue that they were there. Chingo watched the goons join up with Pavielle as they headed to his Hummer. They hopped into the backseat when Pavielle snatched opened the front passenger door. Pavielle was about to duck inside, but then he stopped and turned to Chingo.

"Chingo, if this is a setup, I'm going to crush you and whoever else you love." Pavielle swore behind a mask of seriousness.

"Are you threatening me?" Chingo scowled.

Pavielle lifted his hands in surrender.

"That's notta threat," he told him, "I'm giving you my word."

With that said, Pavielle hopped into the front passenger seat of the Hummer and Gouch whisked him away from the park.

Chingo slid into the driver seat of his Monte Carlo and resurrected it. He pulled out of the parking space and drove out of the park. His cell phone rang and he glanced at the screen. It was just the man he needed to holler at: Paybacc. Chingo pressed 'answer' and brought the cell phone to his ear as he clicked on the blinker to make a right turn.

"What's crack-a-lacking?"

After the conversation with Paybacc, Chingo disconnected the call and placed another.

$$$

Paybacc emerged from the bathroom whistling and zipping up his Dickies. Earlier that night he'd devoured an enchilada plate from Taco Mama with extra chili, cheese, and guacamole. He washed all of that down with an ice cold Heineken. Shortly, he felt his stomach fussing at him and his asshole grumbling. His bowels were eager to be relieved and he was more than willing to oblige them. Now here he was journeying down the hallway patting and rubbing his stomach on the way to the kitchen. He had a slice of cheese cake in the refrigerator that he'd been plotting on before nature called.

When Paybacc entered the kitchen he froze in his tracks and his whistling abruptly stopped. Pavielle was sitting with his red All Star Chuck Taylors propped upon the table and clicking the safety on and off of his .9mm. His eyes were locked in on Paybacc as he twisted a tooth pick around at the corner of his mouth. The windows to his soul were cold and unforgiving. They'd already passed judgment and he was in anticipation of handing down the Death Blow. Paybacc grabbed for the steel on his waistline but nothing was there. That's when he remembered that he'd left it on bathroom sink when he went to take a shit.

A grin emerged on Pavielle's face; he knew he had Payabacc by the balls.

"Have a seat." Pavielle pointed to the chair across from him with his .9mm. Paybacc sat down at the table and he slid a box of Newport 100s before him. Paybacc grabbed the box of Newport's and removed a cigarette. He licked his ashy lips and placed the cigarette between them.

"You gotta light?" He asked Pavielle.

Pavielle fished around inside of his pocket and pulled out a match book. He sat his .9mm down on the table and pulled a match stick from the book. He turned the book over and swept the match stick across the black strip. A flame hissed to life. Pavielle leaned forth and lit Paybacc's cigarette. While he was doing this Paybacc's eyes shifted to the .9mm lying on the table. As soon as he got the notion to grab it he felt movement at his rear. Paybacc didn't even have to look over his shoulder. He knew Gouch and his Girls were right behind him.

Pavielle watched Paybacc closely as he sucked on the end of the cigarette. He went on smoking as if he hadn't had a care in the world. Pavielle reasoned that he'd accepted his fate and would meet it head on, like a man. Pavielle admired and respected that. Paybacc was a gangster's gangster and Pavielle had to salute him.

"Tell Chingo I'll see 'em in hell." Paybacc mashed the cigarette out in the ashtray.

"Will do," Pavielle responded.

Pavielle looked to Gouch and gave him a slight nod. With the signal given, Gouch placed one of his Girls to the back of Paybacc's skull. He wore the face of a killer; solemn and unflinching. His eyes were unforgiving.

Boc!

Chingo was posted outside of Eddie's house, snorting cocaine from off his fist and leaning against his ride when he heard the first gunshot. He quickly screwed the cap on the vial of coke and looked to the window. He wiped his nose with the back of his hand and four more shots rang. With each shot that sounded a flash of light appeared in the window. Moments later, Pavielle and Gouch came walking out of the house. Gouch went on to procure the car while Pavielle stopped to holler at Chingo.

"We're good?" Chingo asked.

Pavielle nodded and said, "We're good. You have my word. I'ma tell my people to cool it."

"Cool." Chingo replied. "I already told my troopers to be easy."

Pavielle patted Chingo on the shoulder and they went their separate ways. Chingo hopped into his whip and pulled off. He pulled his cell phone from out of his jacket's pocket and placed a call. The phone rang twice before his baby momma answered.

"Hey, Babe," Chingo greeted her excitedly. "Good news. It's all over now. You and the baby can…"

Bop! Bop! Bop! Bop!

Blood and brain fragments splattered against the front passenger's window. Chingo slumped over into the passenger seat still holding his cell phone. The sobs and screams of his baby momma ripped through its speaker. Killa Dre dropped the .38 into Chingo's lap and slipped off the latex gloves. He stuffed them into his pocket and hustled back to his moped. He hopped upon it and revved it up. Its engine squealed and Killa Dre took off.

Pavielle was slumped in the front passenger seat of the Hummer. He watched Killa Dre lay down his murder game through the side view mirror as the Hummer drove away. Once Pavielle saw that Killa Dre had made his departure, he sat up and kissed the gold cross of his rosary. Caressing the cross with his thumb, he stared up at the ceiling.

"You can rest in peace now, Unc." He spoke to the spirit of Gangsta.

THIRTY

Lester, the older cat that Pavielle had contacted for G-thang, Voodoo, and Dip's passports, I.Ds, and Social Security cards had pulled upon the block of the home Pavielle owned out in Ladera Heights. He parked six houses down and executed the engine of the Astro van. Once he secured his .45 automatic into the holster under his armpit, he mashed out the cigarette he was smoking into the ashtray and grabbed the duffle bag from off the backseat. Lester wasn't the least bit surprised when he'd gotten the call from Pavielle. Though he'd urged him to change his mind, he'd known that the young kingpin was a stubborn man. He was set in his ways and it wasn't likely that he'd budge on his decision.

For a few extra grand Pavielle contracted Lester to recover G-thang, Voodoo, and Dip and get them out of the country. Lester was hoping that he had called to order their executions since it had been a while since he'd exercised his trigger-finger and felt that his skills as a hired gun was growing rusty. None the less, he wouldn't argue with the extra thirty grand the kingpin had thrown into the bag for his friends' safe transportation out of The United States. As soon as Pavielle's people made the money drop, Lester rented a van in a dummy name and put the Ladera Heights address into the navigation system. Thirty minutes later he found himself in a community that its people had dubbed The Black Beverly Hills.

Lester had just stepped upon the curb when he saw a SWAT team dash past his line of vision and into the yard of the house he was headed to. He froze in his tracks and watched as they slammed a battery ram into the door until it came crashing down. The next thing he heard was a rush of gunfire.

$$$

"Fuck is Dip doing in the other room?" G-thang asked from where he was sitting on the kitchen counter, a Heineken dangling between his legs. He and Voodoo had been discussing their plans once they fled The United States. They had been so engrossed in their conversation that they'd forgotten all about Dip.

Voodoo took a swig of her beer and shrugged, "I can't call it."

G-thang jumped down from the counter and took another swig of his beer, before sitting it down.

"Let me go see what's up with Blood." He started for the door.

"You tryna run a game of Monopoly?" Voodoo asked.

"That's what's up." G-thang replied. "Let me grab this fool and we can get it in. Yo, set that shit up."

"All right," Voodoo went to set up the Monopoly board.

G-thang stopped at the bathroom door. He called out Dip's name a couple of times and knocked on the door, but he didn't receive a response. He then turned the knob and poked his head inside. His eyes bulged and his mouth came open when he took in the sight before him, "Aww, fuck me! Fuck me!"

Dip was hanging from the neck of the shower head by a black cord. His face was slacked and powder blue and piss dripped from between his legs. G-thang smacked a hand over the lower half of his face. The stench from Dip's defication assaulted his sense of smell without any regard. "Voodoo, come quick, hurry up, Girl!" he dashed over to Dip's lingering form, pulling a switch-blade from his backpocket. He grabbed a hold of Dip's legs and lifted him up, relieving the cord of his body weight. Still holding Dip up, G-thang reached above his head and cut the cord free from his neck. Carefully, G-thang carried Dip's limp body from out of the tub and laid him onto the floor, against his chest. Voodoo appeared in the doorway. When she saw Dip lying lifeless her heart immediately dropped into the pit of her stomach. Her vision became obscured as tears manifested in her eyes.

"Is he dead?" Vayda asked, stepping into the bathroom. G-thang looked up at Voodoo and nodded his head. Voodoo was surprised to see tears sliding down his cheeks. Throughout the hood G-thang was known as a barbarian thug who'd wage war in the name of the set on command. Up until now she had always looked at him as a slab of concrete, void of emotion, but here and now she was proven wrong. Voodoo grabbed a hold of the sink and went to bend to her knees to the floor when she noticed a folded slip of paper on the edge. She picked up the slip of paper and unfolded it.

"What is it?" G-thang asked from the floor.

"I think it's a suicide letter." Voodoo wiped the cascading tears from her face and began to read over the letter.

Dear, G and Voodoo

I know y'all probably saying I went out like a straight up Buster for taking my own life, but I couldn't live another day on this earth knowing that I had stolen the life of that innocent little girl. Please believe me, when I say I struggled with what I ultimately decided to do, but eventually I gave in. I realized that I deserved to be punished. We all do, which is why I called the police, before I removed the shackles that held me to this life.

Seeing this made Voodoo's stomach twist into knots and her heart quicken. She felt like she could vomit and faint all at the same time. G-thang saw the sudden change in her mood and worry seized his face.

"What's wrong?" he asked Voodoo. She handed him the paper and he read over it. He was stunned. "Shit!" he banged his head up against the wall. He then looked to Voodoo. "Blood, we've gotta get outta here."

Boom!

Voodoo and G-thang's head snapped to the direction from where the sound came. They already knew what time it was. The police were there to haul their black asses to jail.

The door rattled for the second time, from the police trying to get it.

"What're we gonna do, G?" Voodoo asked, staring out of the bathroom at the front door.

"I already told you, Girl, I'm not going back to the pen." G-thang reminded her. "On The Blood B; they're gonna have to carry me outta this mothafucka inside of a bag."

Voodoo dashed out of the bathroom and returned with their guns. She passed G-thang his weapon and he chambered a round into the head of it. Together they made their way into the living room. They stood side by side, bangers hanging at their sides.

"I love you, Bro." Voodoo told him.

"I love you too, Voo." He embraced her with his free arm and kissed the top of her head. They shared their moment and then…

"Alright, enough of that soft shit!" G-thang broke their embrace. "These mothafuckaz are gone give us a gangsta's death."

"Two sho'," Voodoo replied.

G-thang and Voodoo pointed their bangers at the door. Their hearts pounded inside of their chests as they waited for the front door to come crashing in.

Boom!

The front door came crashing down to the floor and there the police stood with their weapons aimed to kill. Voodoo and G-thang released war cries and unleashed the fury of their weapons. Slugs as hot as coals ripped through their faces, torsos, and arms as they fired their tools. They took more than thirty hot-ones before falling to their deaths and even after all of that they still took three cops with them.

$$$

After hearing the rush of gunfire, Lester tossed the duffle bag into the Astro van and posted up beside it. He lit up a cigarette and observed the house from a far. He watched as six dead bodies covered in white sheets were rolled out of the house and loaded into coroner vans. That was all he needed to see to come to his conclusion. Lester pulled out his cell phone and jumped back behind the wheel of the van. The line rang three times before someone picked up.

$$$

Pavielle and Gouch posted up beside the Hummer passing an L between them. A few minutes had passed before Killa Dre and Banga came rolling up in his Dodge Charger. Banga double parked the Charger in the street and the young men approached the older G's. Hand slaps and daps were exchanged amongst the men.

"This shit is finally over Blood." Killa Dre said. "I thought this shit would never end."

"On me, Bleed, I live for the drama but sometimes a nigga needs a break." Banga added.

"So, what's our next move?" Killa Dre inquired.

"Y'all Y.Gs keep holding it down like you been doing." Pavielle told them. "I got it from here. I gotta meet up with this plug tomorrow night. After I get my hands on these pies, we back on in a major way. So, I hope y'all ready to get this money."

"Hell yeah," Banga said.

"A nigga always ready to eat," Killa Dre spoke up.

"Good, 'cause that's the kind of shit I wanna hear." Pavielle took a puff of the L and his cell phone rang and vibrated. He pulled the cell phone out of his pocket, pressed 'answer' and pressed it to his ear. "What that shit do, Les? You pick up my cargo?"

When Lester delivered Pavielle the bad new, his eyes bulged and his mouth hung open. The pain he felt was the equivalent of an arrow piercing his heart. The blunt fell from his mouth and he staggered back like he'd been shot. Gouch, Killa Dre, and Banga looked upon him wearing confused expressions. They didn't know exactly what was going on but they knew that he had been given bad news. Pavielle staggered back until he bumped into a parked Toyota pickup truck. He dropped the cell phone and turned to the Toyota, banging his forehead against it as tears slicked his cheeks.

"No, no, no, no!"

Each time Pavielle's head deflected off of the Toyota it made a bang sound. Slowly, he started punching the front passenger window, gently. And then those punches became louder and harder with each one that he threw. Pavielle was angry and hot. He could feel his blood boiling and rising to the top. He snarled and punched the window as hard as he could, shattering the glass and breaking his hand in the processed. Pavielle staggered back cradling his wounded mitt. He tripped and fell to the sidewalk, lying on his back and bawling.

"Hello! Hello!" Gouch said into Pavielle's cell phone, but no one answered. All he heard was the line hanging up in his ear.

Gouch threw the cell phone and got down on his knees beside Pavielle.

"Booby, what happened? What's going on?" Gouch questioned.

"No, no, noooooooo!" Pavielle bellowed. "I'm sorry, I'm so fucking sorry!"

"What happened, Man? What the fuck is going on?" Gouch asked.

"They're dead, Gucci," Pavielle sobbed. "All of 'em."

"Who?"

THIRTY ONE

The next day

Gouch sat in the driver seat of the Hummer changing the channels on the stereo system. The day had been a long and hard one. He and Pavielle spent the greater part of it dropping off shopping bags of money to the families of G-thang, Voodoo, and Dip for their funeral sevices. Pavielle had spent six hours at the first two houses and was going on his tenth hour at this last stop. Though it was hot as fire that day Gouch didn't dare to put a rush on Pavielle. He was paying his respects to the families of the men and woman that had died in his honor so it was only right that he was allowed time with them. Besides, Gouch would be all right. The A/C made him feel a lot cooler, like a bottle of champagne sitting in a bucket of ice.

Pavielle snatched open the door and deposited himself into the front passenger seat. He slouched down into the seat and fired up a cigarette. He took a casual pull and unleashed white smoke. Gouch could tell that the situation was eating away at him. The pain was etched all over his face. Not to mention, he was sucking on the end of the cigarette like he was a nigga facing life without parole.

"You, all right?" Gouch asked concerned.

"Hell naw, I'm fucked up." Pavielle admitted, dumping ashes into an ashtray. "I need a drink, and bad than a mothafucka, too."

"You tryna hit The Bar Fly?"

"Nah, I'll sulk later." Pavielle told him. "Let's slide up here to see Sazoo."

"All right."

Gouch resurrected the Hummer and merged into traffic.

Pavielle and Gouch engaged Sazoo at Simpson's family mortuary in Inglewood off of Manchester. At first Pavielle thought they had the wrong address but he checked the slip of paper he'd written it on. The address was indeed the right one. But Pavielle wanted to be especially sure, so he called Sazoo and he told him to come to the entrance. Pavielle knocked on the door and a dark skinned cat in a cheap suit answered the doors. The cat stood about 5'7 and looked like a walking corpse. The cat said nothing as he allowed The Hoods Brothers inside and locked the doors behind them. He signaled for them to follow him and they fell in line behind him. He led them through a dimly lit corridor and into a room that had coffins scattered everywhere. Pavielle and Gouch peeked inside and saw Sazoo smoking from a long, wooden exotic looking pipe. Pavielle and Gouch could tell from the aroma of the weed that it was Grade A. The cat in the cheap suit knocked on the door and garnered Sazoo's attention.

"Sir," the cat spoke in a deep, baritone that didn't match his appearance. "Your guests have arrived." He then gave a bow and went about his business.

Sazoo exchanged pleasantries with Pavielle and Gouch. He offered them a toke of his pipe. Though Gouch refused, Pavielle chose to indulge. He needed something to make him forget about his worries.

"Careful now, that's some powerful sheet." Sazoo warned Pavielle.

"I know what I'm doing, Homeboy. I'm not new to this, I'm true to this." Pavielle held the pipe and lit it at the end with a Bic lighter. He took a couple healthy puffs and expelled white smoke.

"You like?" Sazoo asked.

"Oh yeah," Pavielle coughed and pounded a fist to his chest. "That shit official."

Sazoo took the time to take a couple of puffs himself before speaking. "All right now, let's get down to business." He smacked and rubbed his hands together. He motioned for Pavielle and Gouch to follow him as he headed to a couple of coffins at the back of the room. One by one, Sazoo lifted the lids of the coffins and exposed the kilos inside. Pavielle and Gouch looked between both coffins, nodding their heads. They were happy with what they saw before them.

"Dere you have it, Gentlemen." Sazoo said, "Some of da best cocaine on the market; fifty keys, my neegaz."

"Is this the same shit you let me taste in the park?" Pavielle inquired.

"Yes." Sazoo answered, "Now, the money."

Gouch handed Sazoo a duffle bag. Sazoo sat the duffle bag on a nearby coffin and unzipped it. A smile stretched across his pale, yellow face when he saw all of those big face hundred dollar bills.

"You want us to wait while you count it?"

"No. I'm sure it's all here." Sazoo said, outstretching his hand. "Nice doing business with you…I'm sorry, what was your name again?"

"Pavielle, but you can call me, Booby." He shook Sazoo's hand.

"OK, Booby." Sazoo boasted all 32 like he knew something that Pavielle didn't. Pavielle narrowed his eyes and tilted his head to the side.

At that precise moment, several coffins lids came flying open, one by one.

Boom!

Boom!

Boom!

Boom!

Boom!

Men and Women wearing windbreakers with D.E.A emblazoned across the backs of them shot up in the coffins drawing their weapons on Pavielle and Gouch.

"Don't move mothafuckaz!"

Pavielle and Gouch observed their surroundings. Once they came to the conclusion that they were busted, they slowly lifted their hands into the air. One of the D.E.A agents jumped out of his coffin and handcuffed both of the brothers. While he was being handcuffed, Pavielle mad dogged Sazoo with contempt in his eyes.

"Aww, come on now, don't look at me like that." Sazoo said without an accent as he pulled his shield from out of his shirt and let it hang against his chest. "You knew the risks in the game 'fore you joined in it. We're all players, you just so happened to be playing on the wrong team."

Pavielle harped up some phlegm and spat it Sazoo's face. Sazoo smiled and wiped the goo from his face with a handkerchief from his back pocket. Once he'd wiped his face clean his folded up the handkerchief and tucked it into his back pocket.

"Get these pieces of shit outta here." Sazoo ordered the arresting agent. With that said, Pavielle and Gouch were hurriedly ushered out of the room.

THIRTY TWO

Two days later

She sat there before him on the stool, holding the telephone to her ear. Her makeup ran as tears cascaded down her face. The pain she was feeling couldn't be denied.The expression on her face portrayed that. Her eyes were bloodshot and her jaw was slacked. She didn't know what to say, nor did she know what to do. What he'd told her had sent her world off course and spiraling out of control. Her life would never be the same, and how could it without the love of her life? At this very moment, she hated herself for falling in love with someone like him, but she hated him more for making her love him.

"Vay, did you hear what I said?"

"Yeah…" she took the time to wipe the tears seeping from her eyes. "I heard what you said but I'm not leaving you in here to rot."

"Wrong, that's exactly what you're going to do." Pavielle stared her dead in the eyes. "You're going to go on with your life and raise our son, and you're going to tell him all about me. You'll raise him to be a better man than me. You'll show him that these streets are a bitch and once she takes a hold of you, it's hard to shake her loose. You tell him how this lifestyle is addictive and you can become hooked on it, like you can any other drug. Whether it be cocaine, heroin, or whatever...The game is a drug. It provides a high and a thrill just like any other narcotic, and there ain't no rehabilitation for the shit."

"I'm going to do all of that, but I'm not just gonna leave you in here." Vayda said defiantly. "You hear me, Pavy? You're going to be outside of these walls to help me raise this beautiful baby of ours, do you understand?"

For a time Pavielle didn't respond, but then he nodded.

"I need to hear you say it, Baby."

"I understand."

"Good. I'm coming back to get chu, you just be ready when I get here." She told him. "All right?"

"I got chu."

Vayda placed her hand flat on the pleiglas and said, "One life."

From the other side of the Plexiglas, Pavielle placed his hand flat over her's and replied, "One love."

They hung up the telephones at the exact same time. Vayda then rose to her feet and placed a loving kiss on the plexiglass, leaving a purple imprint behind. 'I love you' she mouthed and then he mouthed it back. They then went there separate ways.

Pavielle walked past Gouch on his way to the door that he'd came in through. They exchanged nods and Gouch went back to the conversation at hand.

"Yeah, Blood, old boy was a D.E.A agent." Gouch shook his head. "Agent Leonard Dukes, mothafucka sunk the whole family."

"Damn." Killa Dre said hating to hear that.

"Booby talking about holding the weight," Gouch informed him. "He's gonna try to work a deal for me to walk and him to be left holding the bag. Ain't no way in hell I'm letting him do that. And I'm not letting him rot in this bitch, either."

"What chu gone do, my nigga?"

"What chu think?" Gouch gave him a hard, unflinching look. Killa Dre didn't like the look his big homie was giving him. He had a pretty good idea what he was getting at but he hoped that he was wrong.

"All right, Hood, times up!" A C.O came to stand behind Gouch.

"I'm out this bitch, Killa," Gouch said. "Twenty Gang…"

"…Or don't bang." Killa Dre finished the phrase.

They hung up the telephones and made their departure.

$$$

Banga sat behind the wheel of the Dodge Charger nodding his head and drumming his fingers on the steering wheel as he listened to Rick Ross's Mastermind CD. He had been waiting on Killa Dre to return from walking Vayda and Little Nasheed to the luxurious hotel she was staying in while she was in town. About fifteen minutes later, Killa Dre came strolling to the car. He snatched open the door and planted his ass into the front passenger seat. As soon as Banga rolled out into traffic, he lit up the half of L he'd been smoking on their way to the County jail. Banga stole a glance in his direction and knew that something was weighing heavily on his mind.

"What's popping, Bleed? You've been tight lipped since we left the tombs."

"Something Gucci said back in County. Well, he didn't actually say it; it was more like a look he gave me."

"What chu mean? What were y'all talking about?"

"He and Booby being locked away inside of The Beast for the rest of their lives," Killa Dre answered. "He wore the look of a man willing to do anything he could to set them free."

"So, what, you think he may rat to save their asses?"

"No. I think he may rat to save his brother's."

Banga laughed his ass off then shot a look to Killa Dre. "Gucci? Snitch? Get the fuck outta here! That nigga's the G'est of the G'est. I don't know about your big homie, but my big homie stand up. My nigga much rather dip his prick in a pond filled with piranhas than roll over. If there's any nigga I'm sure of it's that nigga there."

Killa Dre blew white smoke from the side of his mouth and passed the L to Banga.

"I'm glad you're so sure, Homeboy, 'cause I'm not. I've dropped some bodies with that man; I can't gamble on his loyalty." Killa Dre admitted. "For as much as these niggaz out here pop that gangsta shit, there's only a handful of 'em that are going to wear that time, feel me?"

"True dat," Banga nodded.

"Pull over at the lil store right here." Killa Dre directed with his finger.

Banga pulled into the parking lot of a liquor store/ mini mart. Killa Dre fished around inside of the change holder into he gathered up enough coins to make a phone call. After wards, he hopped out of the car and made a beeline to an old raggedy telephone booth that looked like it didn't function. He snatched up the receiver and wiped it off on his shirt and cradled the telephone to his ear. Once he dropped the coins into the slot. He glanced over his shoulder as the line rang.

"What that shit two, B-Man?" Killa Dre spoke into the telephone. "Ain't shit, a nigga straight like six o'clock; listen, are your people still up in County?"

$$$

Gouch sat on the bottom bunk shuffling a deck of playing cards in unique ways as he watched Pavielle brush his hair back into a ponytail.

What're you getting all snazzy for? We're in a house full of cocks." Gouch inquired. "What, you found a nigga you like in here?"

Gouch laughed.

"Nah, I'm going to see the warden." Pavielle said seriously, washing his face in the sink. This wiped the smile off of Gouch's face. He stopped shuffling the playing cards and brought his legs over the bed, allowing his feet to touch the floor.

"For what?"

"You know what for, Big Bro. We've already discussed this."

"Booby, how long have I had your back?" Gouch asked.

"Since the day mom's pushed me outta her womb."

"Right," Gouch agreed. "So what makes you think that I'ma let chu bite the bullet? The big brother looks out for the little brother, that's how it has always been since the dawn of men."

"I know you've always had my back and I love you for it." Pavielle confessed. "And right now I'm about to prove it by brokering this deal. If this goes my way you'll walk out of here a free man and you'll help Vayda raise your nephew."

"I can't rock with that."

"Well, that's too bad. You may not like it now but just as soon as your ass is on the other side of these walls you'll learn to live with it. Then you'll be thanking me."

"Listen, Man…"

Pavielle whipped around, cutting Gouch short, "Nah, you listen, Gregory, for as long as I can remember you'v been pulling my ass out of the fire. Now it's time I pulled out yours. You're gonna shut the fuck up and let me do what needs to be done! Or we can get it from the shoulders right now! The loser will be the one left holding the bag!"

"I don't wanna fight chu, Baby Bro," Gouch raised his hands in surrender, "If this is the way you want it then you got it."

"All right then." Pavielle turned back around to the mirror, checking his teeth for food particles. He was none the wiser to what happened next; Gouch locked his arms around his neck in a Sleeper Hold. Pavielle clenched his teeth and tried to thewart him off but his strength was quickly depleting. He could feel himself weakening and growing sluggish.

"Goddamn you, Gucci, don't chu do this shit to me!"

"I do what I do 'cause I love you."

Pavielle squirmed under Gouch's arms for another three minutes before he was out cold. Gouch placed him into the bottom bunk and covered him with the thin blanket. He then kissed him on the side of the head and approached the door, pounded on it with his fist.

"Yo, C.O."

Shortly, a tall, flabby body correctional officer took his time walking down to Pavielle and Gouch's cell.

"What is it this time, Hood?" he asked, as if Gouch was bothering him.

Gouch pulled a crisp folded $100 dollar bill from out of his sock and slid it underneath the door. The C.O examined the bill, making sure it was authentic as he listened to Gouch.

"I need to see the warden."

"About what?"

Gouch looked around as if to see if anyone was listening before replying, "I know about a couple of murders."

The C.O nodded and hurriedly unlocked the cell's door.

$$$

Gouch strode down the tier wearing a smile across his face, which was odd considering he would spend the rest of his natural life behind brick walls and barbewire fences. In spite of his circumstances he found comfort in knowing that his baby brother would be a free man soon. Gouch made a deal with the D.A. He confessed to over fifteen unsolved murders that he'd commited. These were murders that he'd carried out by himself. He didn't mention any of the ones he'd done with anyone else. There wasn't anyway he was wearing a snitch jacket. His bloodline didn't rock like that. He was a thorough bred, a nigga of a far greater pedigree. He wasn't going to suck anyone into his bullshit. If he was going to go down then he was going to go down by himself.

Gouch knew that Pavielle would hate him for what he had done, but he was sure that he would forgive him after a while. Once Pavielle had Little Nasheed in his arms and Vayda by his side he'd realize what he had done was for the greater good. Gouch had just approached his cell's door when four Mexicans emerged from the cell next to it. They all wore hard faces and gripped shanks the size of Butcher knives. Gouch looked to his rear and four more Mexicans were coming up the tier, they were carrying shanks as well.

$$$

Pavielle slowly stirred awake from the enduced sleep Gouch had put on him. He sat up in bed and peeled open his eyes. He looked around groggily and then it dawned on him what had occured. "Shit." He scrambled to his feet and ran over to the door of his cell. He pounded on it as hard as he could and called for the C.O. He stopped once he saw Gouch approaching, but knew something was wrong from the expression on his face. That's when he saw the Mexicans closing in on him. Pavielle knew that some shit was about to crack off. He twisted and turned the door knob trying to get out so he could help his brother but it was locked. He figured that the best he could do was make enough noise to get the C.O's attention. With that thought it mind, Pavielle pounded and kicked the door with all of his might. His attack on the door grew louder and vicious seeing the Mexican's stabbing Gouch up. Tears escaped his eyes and he felt his heart crumbling, but he ushered on, assaulting the door unmercifully. He hoped and prayed that someone would come and rescue his brother.

$$$

The Mexicans rushed Gouch from both sides, attacking from all angles with the shanks. Gouch tried to put up a fight but his efforts proved futile. The shanks hit hit from every direction you could think of and even after he'd grown limp they kept on coming. Grunts and vulgarities escaped the lips of the Mexicans as they plunged the blades deep into Gouch's body. The sound of metal hitting flesh filled the air and specks of blood clung to the walls and dripped thick upon the floor. Once the Mexicans were done butchering Gouch, they hoisted him up, and threw him over the railing, American Me style.

"Guuuuucccci," Pavielle's screaming ripped through the air. Tears poured down in his face in buckets seeing what had been done to his brother. He saw the Mexicans leaning over the railing peering down at Gouch. Once they saw that he was dead they turned and walked away. The alarm for lockdown blared loud and furiously. Pavielle took a good look at the faces of the men involved in Gouch's murder. He branded their discriptions into the walls of his memory. Come hell or high water, he would get his revenge even if it meant his undoing.

"You're dead, you hear me! Every last one of you bitches are dead, count on it!" Pavielle breathed fire. Spittled flew from his lips and his hot breath fogged up the rectangle window of his cell's door. He placed his back against the wall and slid down to the floor. Placing his face into the palms of his hands, he cried long and hard.

To Be Continued in...

Me and My Hittas 6

AVAILABLE NOW BY TRANAY ADAMS

The Devil Wears Timbs 1-7

Bury Me A G 1-5

These Scandalous Streets 1-3

A South Central Love Affair

Me and My Hittas 1-6

The Last Real Nigga Alive 1-3

God Bless the Trappers 1-3

A Gangsta's Empire 1-4

Fangeance

Fear My Gangsta 1-5

A Hood Nigga's Blues

The Realest Killaz 1-3

The Last of the OGs 1-3

The Streets Don't Love Nobody 1-2

The Dopeman's Bodyguard 1-2

King of the Trenches